P9-DCJ-987

Maddie squared her shoulders and began. "It's time I forge my own path. I'm tired of being the last duckling in line."

His eyes went wide. "Huh? You're not making any sense right now. What on earth are you trying to say?" Axel was looking at her like she was speaking another language, but Maddie would hold her position.

Lifting her chin, Maddie said, "You're right. That analogy won't make sense to anyone but me. So let me use two words I know you'll understand." She took a deep breath. "I quit." She exhaled.

Axel gasped, but she ignored him and pressed on.

"I'm handing in my resignation. Being the professional that I am, I am giving you ample time to find a replacement. Consider this my two weeks' notice."

After uttering the words, she lifted her chest, feeling a sense of relief and freedom. Like she had taken off a dress that was two sizes too small and could now breathe. And she should be able to, having just decided to unload 230 pounds of male off her small shoulders.

Lunging to his feet, Axel touched her forehead. "Are you serious? Or ill? Because you're not making sense right now. A fever would explain your incoherence."

"No. I'm just fine," she said, stepping back and fighting the urge to skip.

Dear Reader,

I am so pleased you chose *Cinderella's Last Stand*. It was so exciting that I was able to continue the Harrington men series from the small town of Love Creek, Florida. I think that Maddie is the kind of heroine with whom a lot of women can relate. She is so much fun and so spunky that it pulled at my heart watching her grow in self-acceptance while finding love. And as for Axel—what a dreamy hero! He has just the right amount of angst that makes my heart swoon. I truly enjoyed watching his character move from selfish to self-realization before he could accept the kind of love that Maddie had to give. I really hope you enjoy their story as much as I did. I would love to hear from you. Please consider joining my mailing list at www.michellelindorice.com.

Best,

Michelle

Cinderella's
Last Stand

MICHELLE LINDO-RICE

HARLEQUIN
SPECIAL
EDITION

If you purchased this book without a cover you should be aware that this book is stolen property. It was reported as "unsold and destroyed" to the publisher, and neither the author nor the publisher has received any payment for this "stripped book."

HARLEQUIN®
SPECIAL EDITION™

ISBN-13: 978-1-335-72418-2

Cinderella's Last Stand

Copyright © 2022 by Michelle Lindo-Rice

All rights reserved. No part of this book may be used or reproduced in any manner whatsoever without written permission except in the case of brief quotations embodied in critical articles and reviews.

This is a work of fiction. Names, characters, places and incidents are either the product of the author's imagination or are used fictitiously. Any resemblance to actual persons, living or dead, businesses, companies, events or locales is entirely coincidental.

For questions and comments about the quality of this book, please contact us at CustomerService@Harlequin.com.

Harlequin Enterprises ULC
22 Adelaide St. West, 41st Floor
Toronto, Ontario M5H 4E3, Canada
www.Harlequin.com

Printed in U.S.A.

Recycling programs for this product may not exist in your area.

Michelle Lindo-Rice is a 2021 Emma Award winner and a 2021 Vivian Award finalist. Michelle enjoys reading and crafting fiction across genres. Originally from Jamaica, West Indies, she has earned degrees from New York University; SUNY at Stony Brook; Teachers College, Columbia University; and Argosy University; and has been an educator for over twenty years. She also writes as Zoey Marie Jackson.

Books by Michelle Lindo-Rice

Harlequin Special Edition

Seven Brides for Seven Brothers

Rivals at Love Creek

Visit the Author Profile page
at Harlequin.com for more titles.

For my son Eric Michael and his wife, Jasmyn, who blessed me with my first grandchild. What a gift! Thank you to Sobi Burbano and Fran Purnell, who read my first drafts and gave me timely feedback. Thank you to my editor, Gail, Megan and others at Harlequin who brought my vision to life as well as to my agent, Latoya, who is such a great support. Thank you to my Sister Friends who helped me get my word count up. As always, much love to my own hero, John, and my sons, Eric and Jordan, as well as Siara, Destinee, Devyn, Dezirae, Erin, Erika and Arielle.

Chapter One

*B*oundaries. *Boundaries. Boundaries.* Life was all about boundaries.

Madison "Maddie" Henry told herself this even as she lay in a king-size bed next to Axel Harrington, voted the world's sexiest man for 2022. She turned on her side to see his cognac eyes on hers, her dark skin a stark contrast against his caramel tones. His pearly whites widened into that smile that had made him a heartthrob and hot bae for millions of women.

Except Maddie. She was way beyond the enamored phase. Axel was too self-absorbed for her tastes. Though he was a generous employer. As the action hero's personal assistant, she had received many exquisite gifts—including a personal car and jewelry. Earrings were his trinkets of choice. Maddie had about five pairs—remnants of returned gifts from previous girlfriends over the past three years. She had given a couple to her best friend, Keri Pittman, and regifted the pearls to her mother. Thankfully, her collection had stagnated since he'd been dating Natasha LaRue the past eleven months. They had met on the set of *The Mantis* and had been almost inseparable since. Of his many arm candies, Maddie had to admit, Natasha appeared to be the sweetest—and the most determined to snag Axel and put an end to his bachelor status.

Maddie had tried to warn the other woman not to invest her hopes in Axel. He was too into himself to appreciate any woman, but Natasha, though kind, wouldn't take Maddie's advice. Natasha didn't believe in getting too close with the help. Maddie knew if she did get Axel to commit to a deeper relationship, Natasha would get rid of her. For some reason, the other woman was rattled by her presence, butting in whenever Axel asked for Maddie's opinion or input.

Axel touched her cheek. "I told you the best way to experience this bed was to get in it. Let me know if you want one." He flipped onto his back and folded his arms behind his head.

Maddie did the same, fighting her slight unease at being so close to Axel, breathing in the scent of his Perry Ellis cologne. "I don't need one. It's not like I have my own place here. And, it wouldn't fit in my room at your penthouse."

Due to the nature of her job, she often stayed with Axel at his New York or Los Angeles residences since she was expected to be on twenty-four-hour call. But the last five months, he had gotten…needy. It was like he needed her advice on everything.

Take this bed, for example. Axel had insisted she help him pick out a new mattress. That wasn't in her job description. Maddie had been hired to set his schedules and other things of that nature, not determine the softness of his bed. Yet, here she was in a department store in New York City, stretched out next to him, her curls splayed across the mattress, doing just that while trying to ignore the curious fans.

"It would if you took one of the bigger rooms," Axel pressed. "Or I could buy you a loft or something here in the Big A."

"No, I'm good. I told you, I don't need you to buy me anything—or rather, give me your credit card to purchase my gifts. My condo back home in Love Creek is all I can handle. My auntie Dawn left that property for me, and that's the only reason I hold on to it. I'm barely there as it is, as much traveling as I do. Thankfully, my bestie Keri agreed to live with me since she's a flight attendant and my condo is less than twenty miles from the airport."

To use her mother's words, Maddie should have already moved on from being Axel's assistant to bigger and better. And Maddie would already be there if she had allowed Faran—her mother went by the single moniker—to use her connections to get her a director's assistant position. But she hadn't wanted to achieve anything because of her supermodel mom. Maddie wanted to get there based on her own merit, which was why she kept her parentage to herself. No one knew.

Not Axel, not Keri—no one. And Maddie preferred it that way. For the first time, Maddie hadn't had to endure comments about her plain features or be compared to her mother's smooth perfection. The ruse was easy to keep up, since Faran spent most of her time in France. Maddie also didn't have to see Faran's exquisite face twist at her unruly curls, her fuller figure, her plump lips, before her mother emitted a sad sigh. It was like the incomparable Faran couldn't imagine how she had managed to produce an offspring who was so…ordinary.

Those had been her mother's words to a friend on the phone when she thought Maddie was out of earshot. The only two things Maddie had inherited from her mother, which Faran approved of, were her dark, flawless skin, and her eyes. But there was no denying she was the offspring of her Jamaican father, Paul Henry, much to Faran's chagrin. Faran had dressed Maddie in the most expensive designer garb, as if that would compensate for Maddie's underwhelming presence.

Once she had graduated from Yale, Maddie had begged her mother to cease with the one-of-a-kind shoes and wardrobe, but every other month, a new box arrived. After a while, Maddie found herself looking forward to seeing what was inside. Particularly the shoes, which gave her a Cinderella-like vibe.

Maddie tugged on her plaid skirt and pushed her glasses up the bridge of her nose. "Can I get up now?"

she asked. "I only agreed to do this because you said you'd look at my script."

"Of course," Axel said, waving a hand before also sitting up. "So do you think I should purchase this one?"

"Yes. This is the one."

"Great." Axel scooted to the edge of the mattress and gestured to the sales clerk. The older woman scurried over to take his credit card.

"We'll have it delivered this afternoon, sir," she said, preening.

Maddie rolled her eyes. The clerk had to be twice his age, but it appeared no one was immune to Axel Harrington. Maddie reached for her tote and pulled out the script she had printed before coming to meet up with Axel. She smoothed the pages and gathered her courage. Then she click-clacked her way over to where Axel stood.

Yes, click-clacked. She wore a retro red shoe with a chunky wooden heel that resembled a mouth with wooden teeth. The glitter drew attention to her feet, but better her feet than her face.

Maddie straightened. "I brought my script for you to look at." She spoke under her breath, wishing her heart would pump at regular speed.

Axel nodded. "Okay. I'll get to it. What's it called again?"

Maddie swallowed and declined to answer. She had told him the name of her story several times. What was so hard to remember about *A Summer's Dream*? Disappointment whirled within her, and she pursed her lips before shoving the papers back into her bag.

Axel must have seen her expression, because the minute they left the store, he asked, "What's wrong?"

She wiped her foggy glasses and cut her eyes, her fury and resentment building. "You didn't hire me to help with bedding. I just completed my fine arts degree in filmmaking, and I should be vetting scripts and helping you with decisions around your career."

"I know. I was at your graduation." Axel's tone told her he didn't view this conversation as serious. He held open the door for her, and she sailed past him to jump into the dark SUV before putting her glasses back on. Maddie wasn't sure why she hadn't quit. Well, she knew why. Her script. The one she had written for Axel. The role she believed only he could play.

But he wouldn't give her a chance.

Axel slid in beside her and gave her a light jab. "Don't get all huffy on me. We have a two-hour drive to the airport ahead of us because of traffic, and if you're upset with me, it will make this an even longer ride. How about I stop by that doughnut place and get you a box of doughnut holes?"

The ones with the jelly filling were her weakness, but Maddie wasn't about to be distracted. She lifted her chin. "I'm good."

"Uh-oh. I know that means you're not good." Axel cocked his head. "What can I do to make things right between us? I can't take it when you pout."

It was only because she detected sincerity in his voice that Maddie decided to take a chance and be truthful. "You can stop texting me at all hours of the day, telling me you have an emergency when you don't."

He wiped his palms on his jeans and nodded. "I can do that. In my defense, choosing my new mattress is sort of an emergency. If I don't get ample rest, then I'll be cranky and I might lose an important role." He raised his brows. "That is related to my career, which is where you, as my assistant, come in." He gave a satisfied chuckle.

Maddie groaned. She didn't know why she even bothered to express her dissatisfaction. The man used his brains to reason away his selfishness. She had done her research—Axel Harrington was brilliant, with a photographic memory. However, he had shunned a career in nuclear biology in favor of capitalizing on his ridiculous good looks and body. Why? Because it was easy. That was her deduction.

It was her fault for refusing the internship with a young, upcoming female director and staying in this job. But she had been thinking of her script. A script into which she had poured her dreams, her passion, her hopes. A script that could change her life, her station—her mother's opinion.

The driver swung into the farthest lane, honking at the drivers glaring at him, and made his way toward the Lincoln Tunnel. There was a light drizzle, and the drops hitting the glass looked like little splatters of tears. It had rained every day that week. Maddie's lips curved. She loved the rain. It hid many of her tears and, when it passed, left her feeling renewed.

She released a deep breath and continued the conversation.

"I need you to respect my time and my space," Maddie said. "I go on vacation in a few weeks, and I need your word that you will allow me to enjoy my time away from you. I need to recuperate."

"I will. I promise. No interruptions." He gave her a calculating glance. "Where are you going?"

"I'm not telling you," Maddie said. "I don't need you showing up with your hive of fans." She reached into her tote and pushed the script into his hands. "What I do need you to do is keep your word. And read my script."

A couple of women had their bodies hanging out the window of an adjacent car, screaming Axel's name. They both wore tanks that barely held up their heaving chests. Lots to see. Axel gave a little wave and his signature grin before turning away from them. Then he reached into the pocket of the seat and pulled out his cap and signature shades.

"I told you to get a darker tint," she said through her teeth when the women continued to holler, asking if he wanted their number.

"I should have listened to you," Axel said. He quirked his lips. "See what happens when I don't listen to you or make a decision without you?"

A yellow light loomed ahead, and the car next to them accelerated, taking the zealous women with it. Their driver stopped at the light. More fans had spotted Axel, screaming for him to look their way.

Maddie rested her head against the window and

drummed her fingers on the door handle, fighting the urge to open the door and race for the subway. "Three weeks, Axel. I need it."

Axel patted her hand before curling his long brown fingers around hers. "You've got it. I won't bug you. I promise."

She faced him. "I mean it. Unless you're in an emergency room hooked up to a ventilator, no 9-1-1 texts."

He saluted. "Even if my leg is broken and it's being eaten by a vicious mama bear, I promise I will not call you."

Chapter Two

Axel Harrington gazed into the earnest eyes of the woman dubbed "America's rose" and willed himself to utter the one word she yearned to hear. She knelt on one knee on the plush checkered rug, a soft smile etched on her face, expectant—having just proposed. On their one-year anniversary. On national television.

Axel and Natasha, his partner on and off the screen, had appeared on *The Drew Barrymore Show* to promote their upcoming film when she slipped to the floor, not caring that her sheer white linen pantsuit would be crushed, to ask for his hand in marriage. Axel knew she fully believed he would go along with her scheme. Her manipulation. And, normally, he would have. He would have allowed Natasha to have her way. He opened his mouth, but it was like the Incredible Hulk had a hand around Axel's throat. The words refused to squeak past his windpipe.

His mind raced, urging him to say yes. To save face. After all, as an actor, he was used to pretending. He was used to tossing out the words *I love you* with just the right amount of emotion to make the ladies swoon. But this wasn't acting. This was real life.

His life. His choice. And Natasha was trying to take that away from him.

Several tense seconds passed.

He could feel the heat of the lights and the sweat beads on his forehead. Drew's grin was frozen in place. The audience, which had been cheering, had hushed.

The cameraman had moved closer into Axel's personal space to capture the moment. Axel thought about their fans, enthralled with their relationship, begging for them to be together, imagining the beautiful babies they would make. The pressure.

Natasha tugged his hand, turning her head to meet Drew's gaze. He hated seeing the pity in Drew's eyes. Then Natasha pinned her light brown eyes on him. Her brows furrowed, and she shook her head. "Don't do this," she whispered, her voice cracking.

He didn't want to.

But he had to.

He had to be true. Even if it hurt. The fact was, marriage wasn't for him. His biological father had walked out on his mother, leaving her alone to take care of a young son, without a reason or explanation.

Running was in his DNA. He wasn't about to enter into that sort of commitment with anyone.

"I'm sorry," Axel said, touching his chest. "I can't." He bent over to help her stand, but she shied away from him. Axel braced himself for her fury, her flashing eyes and cutting words. But they never came.

Natasha lowered her chin to her chest and closed her eyes. Tears spilled through her lids and streamed down her face, and she released soft sobs. The crowd seemed to release a harsh breath, and the boos came at him like a tidal wave. His shoulders bent, and he turned his back to the stage. A couple minutes ago, all was right—he'd been surfing through life, surrounded by blue skies and sunshine. But Natasha's proposal had caused him to wipe out, and now he had to fight to keep his head above water. To breathe. Remain focused. On his movie. The one he was here to promote. Not get a fiancée. But it was impossible to think past the ensuing crescendo.

The hate from the audience was real. Even the cameraman had backed off, giving him the evil eye.

Axel had said no to the hottest, sweetest actress in Hollywood. In front of the whole world. He knew this would go viral and become a PR nightmare. Axel needed his film to do well if his career was going to go the way he wanted it to go, where he could take on more heartfelt roles. He was ready to leave the action-hero world and challenge himself—become more than a face and biceps.

Drew slipped from her armchair to embrace Natasha before facing the camera. She didn't even look

Axel's way. "We'll be back after the break. I can't wait for you to meet a bunch of sisters with some serious singing chops, The Petals."

As soon as the camera stopped rolling, madness ensued. From the corner of his eye, he saw Drew usher Natasha off the stage. The atmosphere was one of chaos, with assistants running in every direction in a panic. All he had done was turn down a proposal, not start a war. Four women dressed in skintight jumpsuits passed him with heat in their eyes and wrath emanating from their bodies.

"That was grimy," one uttered, shoving past him.

Axel rubbed his temples. Things were getting uglier by the minute. His publicist rushed toward him. "What did you do?" Joni asked, blinking rapidly. "Why didn't you just go along with it? Your movie could flop because of this."

He held up a hand. "You expect me to lie?"

She gave a terse nod. "Yes. Lie. This isn't about you. Hundreds of people worked hard to bring *The Mantis* to life. They need the bonuses you promised once the film becomes a blockbuster."

He tugged on his chin. "I'll talk with Natasha. We'll go out in public, share a few laughs. Maybe she'll agree to say this was a stunt."

Joni pointed in the direction Drew and Natasha had gone. "No one with eyes and a heart will believe that was a stunt. Natasha fell apart on the floor crying." She pulled up her phone and gasped. "It's all over social media. People are coming for you." She swiped the screen with rapid strokes, hyperventilating.

Axel dug into his jeans for his phone and dared to look at his social media account. His eyes went wide. The threats. The venom. Wow. He had to get out of there. Axel called his driver and asked him to pull up to the rear of the building.

Joni stopped him. "Where are you going?"

"Love Creek. Home to my mama. Where else can I go?" He was sure his home in Los Angeles and his penthouse here in the city were surrounded by reporters or hovering helicopters.

"Not there. They're sure to hunt you down at your mother's house."

He had six brothers, each with their own place. He could bunk with one of them.

His publicist kept scrolling. Her mouth dropped. "You'd better get going. Some of Natasha's crazy fans are talking about coming here to the studio. I'll get you a private jet. Have your assistant pack a couple bags and meet you at the airport." Her high-pitched voice went nasal.

His legs felt wooden, and he resisted the urge to panic. In the age of free choice, you'd think he had the option to say no. But no one said no to Natasha. Not if they expected to survive. Her fans were notorious about protecting their precious rose. A petal had fallen after his rejection.

Yes. They were coming for him. Still. He couldn't find it within him to regret his response.

"Maddie's on vacation. I'll do it myself," Axel said.

"Vacation?" Joni's brows raised, and she asked the question like she didn't know the meaning of the word. "There's no vacation for the underlings in this business. Fine. I'll go get your bags. In the meantime, try to stay under the radar." She hurried past him, her legs pumping as fast as she could move, considering she had just begun her third trimester of pregnancy.

Axel had begun walking toward the exit when he heard his name bellowed. Drew Barrymore came up to him and tapped his arm. "Why don't you stay and share your side on the show?"

He shook his head and stuffed his hands in his pockets. "Not a good idea."

"Maybe we could spin this. Natasha might come back on air."

He raised a brow. "Really?"

Drew chewed her bottom lip and shook her head. "I figured you could talk to her."

"Trust me, I'm the last face Natasha wants to see right now. Thanks, Drew. I know you mean well, but you've got to get back on air."

The Petals were almost done singing. Drew glanced at her watch before skittering back to the set. He pushed open the rear door and jumped into the SUV, relieved that his driver had been waiting. The flash of the cameras alerted him of the media's presence. Axel fired out directions to the airport and held on to the door when the driver tore off at high speed.

Thirty minutes later, Axel thought of his family and unlocked his phone to check for messages. His mother had already sent a text to their family chat asking if he was okay and offering her home as a refuge. He studied her most recent picture, of a blunt cut with a mixture of browns and blonds that blended well with her skin tone, the color of honey. He couldn't ignore Tanya Harrington or she would come looking for him. His mother stayed fit, so he didn't second-guess her ability to take him down if needed. Axel quickly replied.

Look outside. Is the press there?

Yes. Sorry, His mother texted back.

His response was a shrugging emoji and Call soon.

He wasn't surprised. Love Creek was a small town in Florida. It didn't take long for the press to swoop in like vultures, sensing the probable imminent death of his box office hit. He shuddered. He was becoming as dramatic as his publicist. Axel watched the three dots, signaling someone in the group was responding.

Several pings from his brothers hit his phone, inviting him to hunker down with them. The first was from Lynx, the soon-to-be newlywed. Next, Hawk reached out, but as a professional football player, Hawk was just as famous as he was. The rest of his brothers offered as well, but each one followed up with texts stating that the press was outside their homes. Capturing a photo of him would mean a big payout because of this scandal, so Axel understood why the paparazzi were circling each of his siblings' properties. Axel thought about going to Thailand or somewhere remote but dismissed that idea. He wanted to be near his family, even if he couldn't be with them.

Maddie.

He could call Maddie. No one would think he would venture to her condo. It would be the perfect hiding place until this died down. But she was starting her vacation this week. And he had given his word not to call unless he had a life-or-death emergency.

This potential hit to his livelihood was an emergency. It could be the death of the film—and his career.

His agent called. Ralph Patterson spewed harsh words, bellowing into Axel's ear. "Turning down Natasha was a huge mistake. She is an heiress, practically American royalty. What were you thinking?"

"That I wanted to make my own choice about who I marry," Axel said with steel in his tone. He wasn't about to remain on the defensive about a decision that could impact the rest of his life. "Marriage is important to me. If I got married, I would want it to be for a lifetime."

"Then you'd be the only one in Hollywood. It would have been nothing to drop a couple million on an engagement ring. At least she'd have a bauble to ease her pain."

"Wow. Are you listening to yourself?" Axel shook his head. His agent was ruthless, and when it came to movies, that served Axel's purpose well. But his personal life, not so much. He yelled into the phone. "You handle my business affairs, nothing else. You got that?"

"You might not have a business to handle soon," Ralph said and cut the call.

Axel looked at his phone, tempted to call and fire

Chapter Three

"It must be important," Maddie said, looking at his name on her vibrating phone, playing to the tune of "The Addams Family." She stood in the doorway of her three-bedroom condo, her carry-on between her legs. She had popped home to pack for her vacation. "It has to be for Axel to call, knowing I'm supposed to be on vacation this week. He gave his word."

The sun beamed on her back, making her appreciate the cool air in front of her. Her AC was ticking and humming while keeping her place cool. A sound Maddie appreciated. It was already close to eighty degrees, and the temps were expected to climb to ninety by 4:00 p.m. that day. Maddie had dressed in a yellow romper with a matching pair of sandals, which featured a sculptured heel and suede buckles, but she had slipped a black cardigan in her tote in case the mosquitoes came out.

Keri strutted down the narrow hallway, her carry-on clanking behind her on the wooden floor, coming to join Maddie by the open door.

"His word is as firm as water. You can't be seriously thinking about answering his call," Keri scoffed, putting a hand on a slender hip, irritation evident in her tone. She was close to six feet tall, dressed in a pair of shorts, a billowy blouse and bedazzled flip-flops. "You know he's not calling for anything important. He probably wants something dumb, insignificant, like shoe polish or tweezers." She flailed her hands. "Who knows! Let it ring."

Keri's fascination with the movie star had dimmed once she had witnessed his thoughtless behavior. She urged Maddie to quit almost once a week.

Sweat beads formed across Maddie's forehead and upper lip. She rocked back on her heels while she debated if she should accept the call. The phone stopped its jerky movements, going to voice mail. She released a plume of air.

It rang again.

Maddie tapped her foot and stared at her phone.

"I know that pensive look." Keri shook her head. "Please don't allow Axel Harrington to intrude on the first break you've taken in two years. Two years, Maddie. You promised we were going to Spain." She tucked a long auburn strand behind her ear. "We've been planning this vacation for months. You made it outside the door. All you have to do is ignore that selfish man and we can be on our way."

Her friend was right on so many levels, but Maddie couldn't disregard the ringing phone. "Let me just check," she said, accepting the call and placing the phone on speaker.

Axel emitted a loud sigh of relief that echoed in the entryway. "I'm so glad you answered. I've been trying to reach you for the last three hours."

"I knew it." Keri clenched her fists, visibly trying to control her outrage. Her green eyes held fire.

Maddie stepped over the threshold, taking her luggage with her. She tucked it into the corner and asked, "A cell tower got hit, so my phone was off while they worked to repair it. What's wrong?" She ignored Keri's mumblings to hang up the phone and took it off speaker.

"Ugh," Keri roared, looking upward. "I knew it was too good to be true. Tell Mr. The World Revolves Around Me we have a flight to catch."

Maddie placed a finger over her lips, but Keri wouldn't be quieted. She covered her free ear and tried to focus as Axel rambled on about his interview with Natasha that had taken a bad turn. She listened with half an ear, mouthing to Keri she would be three seconds, max.

In a huff, Keri stomped through the door. "I'm going downstairs to look out for Rochelle," she said, giving Maddie the evil eye. Rochelle was Keri's co-worker and Maddie's friend by association. She gave

Keri a nod and attempted to concentrate on Axel's words.

"I can't go to my home or my family's homes. I wanted to ask if—"

She cut him off, heading into the kitchen to grab an orange. She hadn't eaten that morning. Just then the AC let out a squeal. She frowned. It sounded like she had pigs running around in her unit. Maddie spoke louder so she could be heard over the noise.

"A bad interview is not an emergency, Axel." Shutting the front door to keep out the flies, Maddie walked a few feet into the large living room area and sat on the microfiber couch she had purchased from Ashley HomeStore.

"Have you been on my social pages?" he shot back, his tone sounding incredulous. And frazzled.

"Yes, Axel, because my vacation time is all about you," she said, affronted at his narcissism. "Emphasis on the word *vacation*. I've been planning this trip for ages. You know this." She put her phone on speaker again and jabbed her thumb into the fruit to peel it with her hands. The juice flowed all over her fingers.

He released a heavy breath. "I know it's your time off, and I'm sorry to interrupt—"

"Are you? 'Cause, I mean, if you were sorry, you wouldn't interrupt." She bit into a piece of orange, not even trying to hide her exasperation. It occurred to her that Axel, no matter how self-absorbed, was her employer, so she needed to change her tone. But then she dismissed the thought. If he didn't like her attitude, he could fire her.

She saw a notification that Keri was calling and sent a text that she would be down in a few.

Rochelle and the Uber are here. If you aren't here in three seconds, we're leaving was Keri's response.

Maddie sent a thumbs-up emoji, then groaned. That made it sound like she was okay being left behind, and now she had juice on her phone. Reaching for a paper towel, she wiped her screen. Meanwhile, Axel was still talking. She had to end this call.

"This is different," Axel said. This time there was no denying the mild hysteria in his tone.

She tossed the paper towel in the trash and paused for a beat. Axel always maintained his cool. Her brows furrowed. Maybe... No. She shook her head, and her annoyance surfaced. He was trying to suck her into some frivolous task or errand. "What is it this time?" she found herself asking, hating that she did. That was a sure sign that Axel was beginning to suck her in.

"Natasha proposed to me on air and I...I said no."

Maddie's eyes went wide. She gripped the phone to keep it from falling out of her hand. "What?"

"Yeah, I thought it was a stunt at first, but she meant it." He exhaled. "When I turned her down, she broke. On live TV. But how can I marry someone I don't see myself with forever? At least, I don't think so." His confusion tore at Maddie's soft heart. "Everybody's coming for me. It's a mess right now, and I can't go home because the press is camped out at my place—and my family's."

That was no surprise. Axel might be the world's

darling, but there was no winning against Natasha and her hive. Her fans were serious. But Maddie needed to keep her stance. She was on vacation. From Axel, his world, all this. Spain was calling. And so was Keri.

"I'm sorry this is happening to you, but I suggest you call your publicist. Let Joni help you. That's why she earns the big bucks. I have a plane to catch." Maddie looked at her watch and shot to her feet. She had to get going. She snatched her luggage and scurried to the door, anxious to get off the phone. Just as she put her hand on the doorknob, Axel spoke.

"Maddie, wait…" She heard him take a deep breath before he whispered, "I need you."

His desperation stilled her. Frozen. Her heart raced. The urgency in his voice sent off an alarm in her senses. Axel had never uttered those words that way before. In fact, she couldn't recall him ever saying he needed *her*.

Slowly, her hand fell. In a tone laced with sympathy, she said, "What do you need?"

"I need a place to stay. For a few days. Just until all the frenzy dies down."

She shook her head. "Go to the Ritz, or that spot in Thailand you like."

"Can I stay with you?" he asked. "I need to be somewhere no one would think to look for me."

For some reason, his words pierced her gut. "Why? 'Cause I'm not one of the beauties you date?" She knew she was plain, but goodness, she wasn't a walk-

ing horror show. "Go ask one of your groupies." She
cut the call and sent Keri a text.

I'll meet you at the airport.

I know what that means, Keri returned with crying emojis.

I am coming!!!

Right after she sent that response, the AC emitted
what she could only describe as a sigh. Then all went
quiet. Thank goodness.

Axel called her on FaceTime. She grunted and answered, but only because she knew the man was relentless.

He continued the conversation by answering her
question. "This has nothing to do with your looks,
or lack of, or whatever you mean." He was so into
himself that he didn't even notice that she was looking like a hot mess. "What I meant was your being
my assistant works in my favor. No one would think
I would be with you."

Axel's explanation was insulting, belittling on
many levels, but she didn't have the breath or the
patience to explain further. Besides, he wasn't done
pleading. "Please, Maddie, I won't be but a couple
days, and then I will personally fly you first-class—
no, make that via private jet—to your undisclosed
vacation."

Maddie swallowed the inexplicable hurt and studied him. His eyes were wide, and he looked frayed.

Maddie felt herself caving.

She was sorry. She was pitiful. And Keri was right. "I'm a pushover," she said, curving her shoulders. "Fine. You can stay. But only for a few days. How long before you get here?"

He threw her a grateful kiss. "Thank you, Maddie. I'm so glad you agreed, because I don't know what I would do." She walked to the windows and parted the teal curtains. A white SUV with dark tinted windows pulled into the lot. *That had better not be him,* she thought, even as he said, "I'll be there later tonight."

Maddie's chest heaved. "So, you just knew I would say yes." This man had a lot of cheek, as her Jamaican father would say.

"No, I hoped. I hoped," he said, sounding relieved.

"I'm only sticking around long enough to hand you the keys, and then I'm out of here. You're on your own."

"But I can't be seen," he said. "What if I need something?"

"Not my problem."

"What if I take you to Spain for a month once this all dies down?"

Predictable response. She sighed. "It won't be the same. I want to go with my friends, not my boss. I've been planning this for a while, and I need this time off."

"I can be fun."

She curled her fists. "I'm wasting my breath. You're

not hearing a thing I'm saying. I'll see you when you get here."

Maddie pressed End and ate the last bit of the orange. Axel just didn't get it, so she didn't know why she had even attempted to explain. Needing to wash her sticky fingers, she grabbed hold of the old spout with such force that it broke, causing water to spray her in the face and hair.

"Noooo," she yelled out, reaching under the sink to turn off the main pipe before wiping her face. The front of her shirt was also soaked.

She called the maintenance office who informed her that the plumber was swamped and might not get to her repair until Monday. With a groan, Maddie went to restore her hair to some level of decency.

Something else registered. She stilled. The AC was uncharacteristically silent. Had it died? She walked under one of the vents and held up a hand, praying for cool. But all she felt was warm air.

Oh no. First the spout. Then the AC.

Maybe she wasn't meant to leave.

She texted Keri to let her friend know about the spout and the AC and that she couldn't make the trip. Then she called a few HVAC technicians until she found one who promised to arrive within thirty minutes.

Hours later, Maddie had a new unit and an exorbitant bill, but she was grateful because she couldn't survive a night without central air.

Maddie looked outside into the parking lot. Axel had texted that he was a few minutes away.

She saw his long, powerful legs step out of a black vehicle. Axel had the phone crooked between his ear and shoulder, carrying what looked like an oversized duffel bag.

"You won't regret this," he said once she let him inside.

"Impossible, because I already do," she said, stepping out of view. "I already do."

Chapter Four

The only regret he had was that he had promised Maddie he wouldn't sleep in the nude. Before she had allowed him to enter her home, Maddie had made Axel promise not to do that. And for the past two and a half days, he had kept that promise. Lying on the full-size bed in the small spare bedroom, Axel folded his arms under his head and looked at the ceiling, eyeing the stucco design, trying to be still. Remain cool. His long legs dangled off the bed, and he had hit his left ankle while moving around. Tucking his legs under him, Axel shifted to his side.

The clock on the small oak nightstand said 1:10 a.m. His shirt was damp with sweat, and the flannel pajamas clung to his body. Maddie had insisted on putting on the heat, just because the temp outside had dropped to the low sixties. She might have done that on purpose to annoy him into finding another hideout. After a few restless minutes, Axel tossed the comforter on the floor and fluffed the pillows before stripping off his pants.

Ugh. That didn't help much. His body was over-heating. Axel wiped his forehead with the back of his hand. What he needed to do was open the window. But Maddie had told him she didn't want to chance any spiders or any other critters getting inside. And Axel couldn't chance being seen or recognized.

His shirt joined the pants on the floor.

Now, if only he could sleep.

A cacophony of chirping crickets and frogs filled the quiet hours of the morning. He was an insomniac, but usually it was only when he was in character for a movie. Axel's brain and body would refuse to rest until the last scene wrapped. Then he would hide away and sleep for days.

Besides the heat, the events from The Drew Barrymore show gnawed at him. Axel had replayed the scene in his mind over and over, wishing he lived a normal life. One where he wouldn't be viewed as a pariah for making the right choice. And it had been right, no matter what Natasha or the rest of the world believed. He picked up his phone off the nightstand and scrolled through several apps. Seeing his face splattered across social media, across international waters, and reading the vitriol chilled him. Made him shiver despite the heat. Made him question the lifestyle he had chosen. Made him angry.

These people didn't know him. He was more than the world's sexiest man. More than the action figures he played. He had feelings.

Several times, Axel had typed in a scathing response to someone's comment but he hit the delete button. His father's advice had come back to him—"Before you hit Send, think." Patrick Harrington had adopted him when he was three years old and had been the only father Axel had ever known. And, thankfully, Patrick had been one of the good ones. Axel didn't have any sad-stepchild stories. Instead, he had been raised with love. Lots of love. Unconditional love. From his single mother, Tanya, until she had married Patrick Harrington. And he had even more love from his six brothers. Which was why he couldn't settle for anything less than love.

Speaking of brothers...

Axel pulled up Hawk's number and called him. His oldest, pro footballer brother was also an insomniac.

Sure enough, Hawk answered. "Can't sleep?"

Axel returned to his back. "Naw. I miss my brand-new mattress."

"That's what you're worried about?" Hawk chuckled. "Never mind that your rep is in the toilet, or your movie might tank under this scandal. Axel needs his beauty sleep."

"Whatever," Axel said. His brothers teased him nonstop about his bougie ways. Axel wasn't going to apologize for enjoying the benefits of his career choice. He worked twenty-hour days for months at a time once he had committed to a role. "You're not the one who has to endure a lumpy mattress and a sore neck in the morning."

"I feel it for you," Hawk said, this time with sympathy.

Hawk was a huge, imposing figure on and off the football field. His sheer size and a facial scar had made the media and fans dub him the Beast of the NFL. Hawk had had his bed specially made to accommodate his size. Both Hawk and Lynx were giants compared to the rest of the Harrington men. There was a good reason for that, as his was the quintessential blended family.

His parents had each had children of their own before they met and married. Tanya had Axel, and Patrick had Drake and Ethan. Then one day, Tanya and Patrick had called Axel, Drake and Ethan into the family room and announced they were going to have more brothers—two white foster siblings they had decided to adopt: Hawk and Lynx.

Axel and Drake, both four at the time, had cheered. Ethan had just turned two, too young to understand, but he had jumped up and down with his brothers. They didn't care that Hawk and Lynx, with their black hair, blue eyes and bulky build, were different. The boys bonded without regard to race. A couple years later, Tanya gave birth to fraternal twins, Brigg and Caleb, completing their family of all boys.

Now they were grown men. With grown-up problems.

Axel placed the phone on speaker and crept outside the room. He probably wouldn't run into Maddie at this hour. "I already took care of the furniture problem, though. I have new furniture and bedding being delivered tomorrow."

"Did you ask Madison if that was okay?"

He opened the refrigerator door and paused. "No... I figured she'd thank me for the upgrade. Especially after her entire kitchen sink needed replacing." He bent inside the refrigerator and took deep breaths, appreciating the cool air on his almost-naked body.

"You're thirty-two years old, the sexiest man on the planet, but you don't know a thing about women." Hawk laughed.

"Quit calling me that," Axel said. "It's been months since *People* put me on the cover of their magazine. Haven't you had enough yet?"

"Nope," he shot back. "I don't think it will get old anytime soon."

"If I remember right, you were also on it."

His brother emitted a groan that sounded like a seal's bark. "Don't remind me. But back to Maddie and asking permission. You seem to take a lot for granted with her."

"How so?" Axel asked. Grabbing a bottle of milk, Axel went searching through the cupboards for a bowl and some cereal—specifically, Cap'n Crunch. With all the commotion, Axel hadn't eaten, and now his stomach was protesting. It wasn't used to being denied.

"You don't ask. You expect," Hawk said. "Fame can spoil you, lull you into thinking everything is about you."

He plopped the bowl on the counter and dug around for a spoon. It landed in the empty bowl with a clink.

"But this week has very much been about me," Axel said, finding the box in the cupboard above the refrigerator and opening it. "I asked Maddie if I could stay here, and she agreed."

Hawk chuckled. "I'm willing to bet a million dollars your showing up inconvenienced her."

Knowing he would be out a million dollars, Axel deflected. He poured the cereal into the bowl, filling it to the brim. "That's neither here nor there. The main thing is that I'm staying here, where no one would think to look for me. They're probably scouring somewhere remote, exotic… Like I said, they're definitely not looking here."

"Wow. Are you listening to yourself?" Hawk asked.

"What?" Axel sniffed the milk and then poured it, splashing some of the contents on the counter.

"Hang on. Drake's calling. Let me connect him."

Holding his overflowing bowl, Axel made his way to the small kitchenette. He ate a good portion before his brothers returned to the call.

He and Drake exchanged greetings before Drake said, "Hawk just filled me in, and I am in full agreement. You don't treat your little lady right."

His brows furrowed. "Maddie's not my…lady. She works for me."

"She's a cutie," Drake said. "All that hair. Those curves. Don't tell me you haven't seen all of that."

"Of course he has. He's got eyes," Hawk joked.

For some reason, Axel didn't appreciate Drake's observations or Hawk's consensus. He felt oddly... territorial. He stuffed his mouth with cereal to keep from voicing that aloud, crunching hard enough to hurt his jaw. Maddie was cute in her own way, but she was his assistant. Nothing more. Didn't mean he liked knowing his brothers were eyeing her, though.

"Speaking of eyes, Maddie's are so unique," Drake continued. "Pity she has them hidden behind those glasses."

"What color are they?" Hawk mused.

Axel shifted, then frowned. What were they talking about? Her eyes were... He swallowed. He didn't know the color of her eyes. She worked with him every day, and he didn't know. His brows knitted. How could he not know?

"I bet you a hundred bucks he doesn't have a clue," Drake teased.

Another hundred bucks he would lose. Axel's chest tightened with an odd sensation, and he had to press his lips together to keep from exploding. His mind raced, trying to recall. They were brown, weren't they? Hard to tell with those glasses... But his brothers could. That irritated him in ways he could never express. "Quit ogling my assistant. She's off-limits," he ground out with an edge in his tone.

"We're just messing with you," Hawk chuckled. "Believe me, we all know how you feel about Maddie."

"Yeah, I bet he's heated right now," Drake chimed in. "Relax. We know better than to try to kick it to her."

"I'm sorry I called you turkeys." His brothers

cracked up. From the corner of his eye, he noticed Maddie hovering near the entrance of the kitchen and uttered a quick "I've got to go."

"Axel's in trouble," Drake drawled.

"Juveniles," he shot back before ending the call. He hunkered down, knowing he was exposed, feeling like a kid caught with his hand in the cookie jar—or, in this case, the cereal box.

"I was hungry," he said, by way of explanation.

She was dressed in a large pajama sleep shirt, which hid all her womanly assets. Not that he was trying to find any. Her feet were stuffed in Goofy house slippers. She shoved her glasses on her face and stomped into the room. Well, if one could call it stomping with those slippers. She was braless, and he could see the outline of a pair of generous breasts. Axel averted his eyes, blaming Hawk and Drake for his momentary lapse in judgment.

"You are so inconsiderate. Talking at the top of your lungs. How am I supposed to get back to sleep? And why aren't you wearing any clothes? Didn't I tell you to remain covered while you're here?" She curled her lips and pointed at him. "I'm not trying to see all of that."

Affronted, Axel puffed his chest. "I was hot. And I'll have you know I get paid thousands to show off this body."

"I didn't write the check."

"I was *hot*. Besides, you've seen me in less than this when I'm on set. So, it's really not a big deal."

His explanation seemed to kindle her fury. "Whatever. It's about respect. But I don't expect you to get that." She stormed over to the counter next to the stove and poured spring water into the electric kettle, mumbling, "Making all this noise. Ridiculous." Then she opened the cupboard and pulled out a hot cocoa packet and a mug.

"I didn't know you could hear me," he said, eating the last of the cereal. He wondered how long Maddie had been standing there and how much she had heard. Her face was hard to read.

"I'd have to be dead not to," she grumbled, flicking the packet back and forth in her hand to settle the mix before ripping the packet open and pouring it into a mug.

"Can I have some?"

She raised her brows. "Really?"

"It might help me sleep," Axel said in a sheepish tone. He cleared his throat. "I'm sorry I woke you."

"You're lucky Keri isn't here, or you would be packing your bags tonight."

"She's too busy relaxing in her new suite in Spain. I had both her and Rochelle's rooms upgraded."

Maddie put a hand on her hips. "I should have known you'd bribe my friends."

Axel laughed. "It wasn't a bribe. It was an apology." One that Keri had accepted graciously once he had sweetened it by paying for her extended stay.

"Whatever," Maddie said, waving a hand. "Money isn't everything." She reached for another packet and mug.

"No, but it does serve a purpose." Like squelching

the anger of Maddie's best friends. As soon as he had entered Maddie's condo, Keri had called. Axel had heard her yelling through the phone and had taken the phone from Maddie to assuage her with his charm. By the time he was off the phone, Keri and Rochelle were smiling and promised not to disclose his whereabouts.

"Leave my friends alone," Maddie warned. "They don't know your generosity is a cloak for some selfish motives."

"Okay, I will." But he felt the need to add, "And my motives aren't selfish. I prefer to use the terminology 'mutually beneficial.'"

"Tell yourself that if it helps you sleep better at night," Maddie scoffed before pointing at the kitchen clock. "Clearly, it doesn't."

Axel stayed quiet about the fact that he had paid for Maddie's roommate to have lodging at the Four Points hotel—the best in town—upon her return back to the United States. He squirmed, thinking about Maddie's words about his "selfish" motives. If he benefited by hiding out longer at Maddie's while Keri lived it up in a hotel, what was the harm? It was a win-win for everybody.

Especially him.

Chapter Five

We know how you feel about Maddie...

Those were the words that messed with her psyche—bringing back feelings of inadequacy she had fought to overcome. All through the wee hours of the morning, until daybreak, Maddie had processed that information. Never mind that Axel hadn't known the color of her eyes. Her one redeeming feature. That she could deal with. Axel couldn't see past his own face on most days. But to tell his brothers to stay away from her...that hurt.

Maddie hadn't meant to eavesdrop on Axel's conversation with his brothers, but he had been so loud that he had awakened her. Hearing his conversation had been unavoidable, but she only had herself to blame for feeling some kind of way at how

Axel seemed to dismiss her as a woman, warning his brothers she was off-limits. Like she wasn't good enough for them. Bully. That had made her prickly as a hedgehog when she entered the kitchen, but shoot, she was entitled to her feelings.

But Maddie wasn't that young girl battling feelings of inadequacy anymore. After she got dressed, Maddie placed her AirPods in her ears, pulled up YouTube and played Lizzo's rendition of "The Beautiful Ones." Standing in front of her mirror, mouthing the words, she wiggled her hips and gave herself a swift pep talk about self-love before leaving her room to tackle the day. Or, rather, the spoiled celebrity sprawled across her extra long chocolate couch like he owned the place. His excuse was that the bed hurt his back and the room was too hot. Of course, she had reminded him that he could find accommodations at a five-star hotel. A reminder he ignored.

It was close to nine that Monday morning and Axel was snoring loud enough to wake her neighbors— if she had any. Both of her neighbors had recently moved.

She eyed the almost-naked man who lay on his side, one leg hanging off the couch, a thin sheet draped across his midriff, and groaned. Yes, Maddie was used to seeing him in various stages of undress, but this was her house, her rules, and he needed to follow them. He had stayed up for most of the night, which meant so had she. After they drank their hot cocoa, Axel had flipped through social media, reading some of the hateful posts. Maddie had nodded along, but her entire mind had been on the words *We know how you feel about Maddie...*

What exactly did that mean? That's what she wanted to ask.

But she hadn't—unsure if she was ready for that answer.

Instead, Maddie had shoved her feelings aside and focused on Axel and his needs. Soothed his ego. Even in her haven, it was all about him. Again.

Tapping her feet, Maddie resisted the temptation to douse him with ice-cold water. Kick him out of her space so she could...breathe. But she was all talk—well, thought. Maddie couldn't ruin the couch she had scoured seven furniture stores to find.

Just then, the doorbell rang.

She ambled over to the front door and looked through the peephole to see a delivery man peering back at her, which made his eyes look like a bug's. "Can I help you?" she yelled through the door.

The slender, wiry man gave her a wide smile and held up a slip of paper. "We have a delivery scheduled for nine-fifteen today," he said. He was way too chipper, and she hadn't had her coffee yet.

She cracked the door open a notch and said, "I'm sorry, you must have the wrong address. I didn't order anything."

Frowning, he rattled off her address, turning the paper for her to read.

"Yes, this is the right address, but maybe the person who ordered it made a mistake," she offered, even as suspicion began to rise within.

"An August Moon called in the order yesterday, and we promised we would be here first thing this morning."

She rolled her eyes, now knowing it was Axel who had purchased something with one of his monikers. He generally used a mash-up of months, seasons, planets, stars or even Greek gods when he wanted to remain incognito. Among his favorites were Apollo March, Artemis Fall, Pluto Ares. Sometimes, he had even had her use fake names—Penelope May, Athena Sun...

Opening the door wider, she glanced outside, and her eyes bulged. There were three other men in the hallway, holding various pieces of dark cherry furniture wrapped in cellophane. The men appeared to be related, and the insignia on their green polos indicated this was perhaps a family business.

Maddie's mouth dropped open. "What is all this?" She squinted. Wait. Was one of them holding a paint can? She shook her head. It didn't matter, because it was all going back.

"We have a bed, a chest, a nightstand and bedding," the slender man said with a heavy Creole accent. "Plus, Mr. Moon paid for us to remove the wallpaper, paint and then assemble the entire room." He inched closer. His assistants had big grins on their faces.

She was right that this was Axel's doing, and knowing him, he had tipped them well.

This was confirmed when one of the other men

said, "Don't worry, it's all been paid for, and we can get this set up for you in no time."

"Yeah, I'm so glad for this order, because business was slow," another man said. Four pairs of eyes were trained on her, like they were playing Ping-Pong and waiting for her to make her next move. She could feel their suppressed excitement in the way they kept shifting from foot to foot, obviously ready to get to work.

The gentleman's smile slipped. "Is Mr. Moon here? He can clear it up. Unless it was meant to be a surprise?" he asked in a hopeful tone. He pulled out his phone. "Let me give him a call."

Seeing the gratitude and eagerness on their faces, Maddie didn't have the heart to crush their elation for a sale. Axel, on the other hand…she was going to chew him out and make him deal with the men.

Maddie held up a hand. "Give me one second." She closed the door and bit her lip to keep from screaming. She marched over to the couch, but Axel was gone. He must have heard the doorbell and gone into hiding, not wanting to be recognized. She found him in her closet and demanded he tell the men to leave, ripping into him for not asking her permission before redecorating her house.

"You know it's not a good idea for me to show my face," Axel said, not sounding the least bit apologetic.

Her chest heaved. "You'd better send them on their way. Where is all stuff supposed to go?"

"I can't sleep in that room," he said. "If I'm going to be here, I need to make it comfortable."

She clamped her jaw to keep from exploding.

If he was going to be here? *If* he was going to be here. Like she had invited him. Like she had begged him to intrude upon her private space.

The cheek. The gall.

Her chest heaved. "This isn't the Ritz, where you can make your demands. This is my home. My territory. And I let you stay here because you said you have nowhere to go, but instead of keeping low, you do something like this."

The doorbell rang again. Raking a hand through her hair, Maddie took several deep breaths. "You need to go handle this." She expelled a plume of air and pushed her glasses up the bridge of her nose. "I didn't even shower, and I know my hair is tangled worse than a bird's nest. I can't believe you."

He took her arm. "I'll make it up to you. I promise. I can't disappoint these men. I'm their biggest sale."

Ugh. Hating her bleeding heart, Maddie caved, walking out of the closet. "Fine. But you are sending everything back before you leave. When will that be, anyway?" She didn't even try to hide her delight at the prospect of his departure.

Axel tossed her a kiss and raced toward her bathroom. "I've got to use your shower. Can't chance running into them," he said, pointing to his bare chest. "This is not a good look right now."

Figured. Never mind that she looked like the Swamp Thing. Maddie scurried to the door and let the men inside her home. For the next three hours, she dealt with the clanging and clamor that came with moving. Axel had arranged for them to take the other furniture and put it in storage.

When it was close to lunchtime, Maddie made a Greek salad and grilled some chicken strips and made a plate for Axel, who was sitting on her bed, watching *Jeopardy!*, his long legs stretched out in front.

Axel had dressed in dark jeans and a blue shirt. His Axe body wash scented the room. She paused. Maddie couldn't remember the last time she had had a man in her bed. There were odd moments, like now, when she acknowledged his fineness—the muscles bulging under his fitted shirt, the washboard abs, that cleft in his chin.

His eyes lit up when he saw the food, and he licked his lips. Her throat went dry watching his tongue leave a trail of moisture on his lips. Those full, sexy lips. She blinked, wondering how she'd forgotten Axel was a sex symbol.

Then he spoke, and she remembered. She went to hand him his meal.

"Thank you so much for bringing me something to eat. It's tough being stuck in here."

Never mind that he was the one who had created this havoc in her home. Axel could only think of his inconvenience. His self-absorption was like an opaque film shielding his good looks. It was always about him.

Still, his presence in her private room made her aware of him, his masculinity. Keeping her eyes averted, she pointed to the folded tray table. He swung his long legs off her bed and bent over to retrieve it, giving her a view of his tight butt.

Goodness. She was ogling her boss. Maybe she needed to take Keri's advice and get on an online dating site, 'cause she was feeling warm and tingly. And it wasn't from the heat, because the vent was pushing out nothing but cool air. Because, of course, she had adjusted the temperature to suit him.

"You're welcome," Maddie said, resting the plate and utensils on the table, disliking her breathy tone. Axel sat on the side of her bed and drew the table close, rubbing his hands. Strong hands. Long, tapered fingers.

"This looks delicious," he said, picking up the fork, his eyes glued to the screen. He opened his mouth and slid a piece of chicken off the fork. Maddie zoned in on every move, her mouth going dry. Axel was too involved with *Jeopardy!* to notice her fascination.

"I'll get you something to drink," she croaked out, rushing out of the room. Once she was in the kitchen, she muttered, "What is going on with you? This is Axel. You know him, so stop acting like his fineness is all brand-new."

It must be because he was in her home. In her space. In her bedroom. On her bed. That must be why this new awareness had flickered to life and was filling her mind.

She wiped the small sweat beads on her forehead. That's it. She needed to pick a random stranger, get a hookup, get laid.

No, she didn't. That was so not her.

But once the men left for lunch, she did shoo Axel out of her private domain, banishing him into Keri's room. However, Axel had branded her space. Her brain had snapped a vision of him, imprinted it into her mind. Maddie knew she had to avoid Axel until she had a mental reset.

The workers returned to finish painting and set up the room, and she stayed busy in the kitchen, doing his laundry and cooking dinner until they left. Axel had suggested she order takeout and use a delivery service, but Maddie enjoyed preparing her own meals when she was home. She liked the process of putting different ingredients together, creating a melting pot, and ending up with something savory. Tonight, she had decided to make lamp chops, roasted fingerling potatoes and asparagus.

The aroma filled her condo, and she inhaled. Her stomach growled. It was close to five-thirty, and the sun was still bright outside. Maybe she would eat outside on her balcony. She knew Axel would stay inside.

By this time, the men had left, and Axel was ensconced in the new bedroom. She had yet to check it out. He had carried his laptop with him into "his" room and had been working on his digitized cartoons, a hobby he enjoyed. Axel was super talented at everything he did. Maddie had asked him about using some of his work in animated films, but Axel hadn't indicated interest. It relaxed him, he had said.

"It smells delicious," Axel said, startling her out of her musings.

"Thanks. Help yourself," she tossed out, heading

to her balcony with her meal. She had served herself small portions, and her mouth watered. Maddie hadn't snacked since lunch, so she was anticipating every bite and the solitude.

To her surprise, Axel joined her, placing two glasses of ice-cold water on the glass table. He went inside and returned with his food. He had piled his plate high and donned sunglasses and a baseball cap. He settled into the chair across from her to engage in small talk. "It feels great out here."

"Hmm…" She nodded, loving the feel of the breeze in her hair, on her neck. The one thing she didn't like about cooking was the heat in the kitchen.

After saying grace, she dug into her meal. They ate in companionable silence, and Maddie found she enjoyed having Axel with her. In fact, once they were done eating, Axel charmed her, asking random questions that cracked her up. They bantered back and forth, and Maddie went to bed that night with a light heart. Maybe she could endure Axel living with her for a few days. That was her final thought before she closed her eyes that night.

And then the news broke.

Chapter Six

Her eyes were a blue-gray. Mostly gray with blue around the edges. And they were surrounded by a fan of thick lashes. How had he not seen that before? Axel lay in his bed with one arm behind his head, having just showered and shaved after completing a few sets of pushups and sit-ups, reflecting on his evening with Maddie. He had been up for an hour, and almost every minute had been spent thinking about his assistant while he exercised.

Drake was right. She was a total cutie. He cracked a half smile. He probably never noticed because, from the time he had hired her, she'd stayed in fussing mode. That's why he had chosen Maddie from the eleven applicants he had interviewed with his agent and publicist. Maddie hadn't been dazzled by his celebrity status. In fact, she had critiqued his last movie, pushing those oversize glasses up on her face and crossing her feet at the ankles. She'd been wearing the craziest pair of shoes he had ever seen.

Unlike the other job seekers, who had been coy and flirty, Axel wasn't worried about getting into any entanglements with Maddie. She had been direct, open and unimpressed with his star status. Her attitude was a replica of his favorite teacher's. And she had been ready to start that day.

Axel had hired her on the spot and had never regretted his decision. They maintained a great professional relationship, and he could rely on her to come through for him every time.

Yet he couldn't get those remarkable eyes out of his mind.

Or her smile. He had enjoyed making her laugh the night before and seeing the flash of her pretty teeth. It was relaxing. He didn't have to be on all the time. He could just be.

Natasha always had a barrage of people surrounding her. He had to be dressed to the max in case they were photographed. It was work keeping up with her image of perfection. Lucky for him, he was confident in his own skin.

A little too confident, Maddie would say. He chuckled before getting out of the bed. After slipping into a pair of lounge pants and an old T-shirt, he traipsed into the kitchen and decided to make breakfast. As the second-oldest of seven siblings, Axel's mother had made sure he knew how to prepare a few staples. All his brothers did, although Ethan and Caleb took preparing cuisine to another level.

He opened the refrigerator and scrunched his nose. The fridge was stocked with meal-replacement protein shakes, containers of leftovers and not much else in terms of breakfast foods. Maddie needed to go grocery shopping. He moved the shakes aside and found eggs and a carton of spinach. He didn't see any milk. Axel grabbed those two items and placed them on the counter and searched for a frying pan, salt and pepper.

Using those four ingredients, Axel whisked together a couple of omelets for himself and Maddie. He had just plated them and gathered utensils when she came strolling into the kitchen.

She wore baggy pajamas, and her hair formed a halo. She didn't have her glasses on, so her remarkable eyes were on display.

"What's all the clamoring about?" she asked before squinting at the food on the counter. "You made breakfast?" she asked, incredulous.

He could smell her minty breath from where he stood.

"Yes. I know how to do a little something, something." He touched his chin. Maybe he could get her in touch with an ophthalmic surgeon. Get her eyes fixed.

She lifted the plate, narrowing those gorgeous eyes at the omelet with suspicion before taking a sniff.

"It's safe to eat," Axel laughed, reaching around her to get his food.

"You've never cooked before." Her tone sounded a

tiny bit accusatory. "In fact, I can recall rushing out to order you this same thing."

He shrugged. "I can't let out all my trade secrets."

"Whatever," she mumbled before shuffling out the room.

Axel placed their plates on the dining table and filled two glasses with cranberry juice. Maddie returned a few seconds later with her glasses on. *What a shame*, he thought.

She pulled out the chair and sat across from him. "Thanks for making breakfast."

"Do you have any plans for today?" he asked.

Maddie held her index finger to her chin and furrowed her brows. "No, my boss is in hiding and I was supposed to be on vacation, so my schedule's all clear. What about you?"

He chuckled. "Good one."

"I plan to watch my fave black-and-whites," Maddie said. "And work on my script."

"Black-and-whites?"

"Casablanca."

Axel raised a brow. "My mother loves that movie. It's actually one of the reasons I decided to pursue acting. Humphrey Bogart is phenomenal."

"He's a classic," Maddie said, nodding. He watched her bite into the omelet and close her eyes. Then she groaned. "This is good."

It was like she was savoring every morsel. His chest puffed, knowing he had a small part in putting that look on her face. Then a traitorous and tantalizing thought wormed its way into his brain. There were other ways he could put that look on her face...

Axel shook his head, shuttering his gaze. He had to divert those wayward thoughts about his assistant. His *assistant*. As in employee. He jumped into talking with enthusiasm with Maddie about their favorite parts of *Casablanca*, which led to them sitting side by side on the couch eating popcorn at ten thirty in the morning while watching Humphrey Bogart and Ingrid Bergman on the screen.

As he had when he watched with his mother, Axel found himself drawn into the film, the acting, the emotions.

"You could do that part," Maddie said in a low voice.

Axel turned to face her. "You think so?" he asked with wonder.

"I know so."

Her confident tone made him lean in to look at her closely. Maybe she was joking. However, her expression showed her sincerity. Maddie looked like she believed he could do a serious role. Axel paused the movie and leaned closer.

"What if I told you that I want to move away from the slapstick humor and superhero characters?" He bunched his fists, his voice filled with passion. "I want to take on meatier roles, make my audience feel something raw. Something real." His heart thumped in his chest at his admission. Axel had never shared this desire with anyone. Well, he had broached the topic with Natasha, but she had shut him down, stating he needed to stay with what worked. Axel had learned to hide his true feelings under humor. He was prepared for Maddie to laugh, like Natasha had.

But she didn't.

"You should," she said, shocking him with her firm, assertive response.

He straightened. "I didn't expect your support."

Maddie adjusted her glasses and then touched his cheek. "There's more to you than a body, Axel. You're self-absorbed, but I don't think you're selfish at heart." Her voice was soft, gentle. "I've always known that you have a true gift. Put yourself out there and go for it. In fact, I have the right script for you, if you're interested."

He felt a zing from the heat of her hand on his cheek and tilted his head away. The feel of her touch was too…intimate. Too tender. Maddie had touched him before, but he had never felt like they connected. Like she understood. It confused him. Made him uncomfortable, and that's not how he viewed his relationship with Maddie.

Then his cell phone rang, throwing him a lifeline. She removed her hand, and he put some space between them. Seeing his brother Lynx calling, Axel answered the phone, putting it on speaker. The brothers exchanged pleasantries before Lynx got to the purpose of his call. He wasn't calling as a brother but as the principal of Love Creek High.

"My drama teacher had to have emergency surgery and will be out for close to a month. We have a massive sub shortage. So, I was thinking that since my brother is this big-time celebrity, maybe he wouldn't mind covering the class? The students are working on a production of *The Sound of Music*, and they would be psyched if you gave them some pointers."

Axel shook his head. "I don't think I want to do that. I'm not trying to attract attention here, and I don't know if I'm ready to deal with moody teenagers."

"You should be, since you were the moodiest of us all. And conceited. Preening before the mirror and flexing your abs."

Maddie snorted and jabbed him in the ribs. "I can see you doing that."

"Hey, Maddie," Lynx called out.

"Hey," she said, leaning forward to speak into the phone. "Your brother needs something to do besides driving me bonkers."

Axel gave her a sideways glance. "Don't listen to her. She's loving every second of me being here."

"If you say so," Lynx teased. "Please say you'll think about it? The drama students are going to be disappointed when I break the news of Ms. Millner's absence. It would lift their spirits to hear that you will be her replacement."

"Aw," Maddie said.

"Ms. Millner's still there?" he said in amazement. She had been his drama teacher and had a fiery spirit and a big heart.

"Yes. I've been begging her not to retire, but after this, I don't know if she'll be back."

Axel felt a tug of compassion, but he wasn't sure he

could lock into any kind of commitment. The thought of dealing with adolescents terrified him. They had no filter. They were honest. And he might suck at directing.

"I'll help if you agree," Maddie offered, brimming with excitement.

"That's wonderful, Maddie," Lynx said. "I appreciate your willingness to assist."

Axel pursed his lips. "Don't try to guilt-trip me. Give me a day to think on it."

"Yes, he's swamped with working out, eating and being a general nuisance," Maddie added, standing to stretch.

His phone beeped, indicating another call on the line. It was Joni. "Bro, my publicist is calling. I'll holler at you later," Axel said and clicked over, once again keeping the phone on speaker.

His publicist was frantic. "Where are you? I called your mother, but she says you're not with her."

"I'm at Maddie's. Didn't you get my text?"

"What are you doing there?" she asked. "The last thing you want is for people to think you two are an item."

"Relax," he said with a chuckle. "You're being overly dramatic for nothing. No one who knows me would believe I'm dating Maddie. She's my assistant, and Natasha knows that Maddie is not the type of woman I usually date. So, I don't think we have anything to worry about even if word did get out that I'm here."

"Fine. Whatever. Remain indoors with the curtains closed," Joni shot back.

"Maddie, tell Joni she is making a big deal for nothing," he said, gesturing to her to back him up.

Axel expected her to sit next to him and chime in, but she leaned against the wall and shook her head. For some reason, she refused to meet Axel's gaze and walked out of the room.

He narrowed his eyes at the cool reception, wondering what had changed her mood. But Joni had begun spouting off about his making another appearance on Drew's show or even late-night television.

"No. I'm not ready to return," he said. "I haven't had a break in over a year. This is a forced break, but I need it." Until Axel had voiced those words, he hadn't comprehended how much he was enjoying his time out of the spotlight.

It was nice to just…be.

Joni released a breath. He could almost feel her strategizing. "Fine. I'll reschedule everything out a few weeks. That will give us a little more time for the ripples to taper off. Then I'm reaching out to Natasha to get her to agree to join you on the tour."

Axel rubbed his head. If he knew Natasha, she wasn't going to allow anything to affect her money. When it came to her career, she was dedicated and all business. "I'm pretty sure she will agree— eventually."

"Have you spoken to her?" Joni asked, sounding hopeful.

"No, she hasn't reached out." And neither had he.

If he was being truthful, Axel hadn't thought about Natasha at all. His mind had been filled with Maddie's eyes.

"Okay. I'll work on that, but in the meantime, you need to stay out of trouble. Maybe visit a hospital, a nursing home, or rescue stray dogs. We need to show there is more to you than bulging biceps. Fluff. We need to show the world you're a superhero in real life as well as on the screen. You're more than a movie star. You're human, normal, like the rest of us." Her voice dropped. "And that you care about something or someone other than yourself."

Her words caught him off guard, slicing him to the core. Was that how everyone saw him? With sudden desperation, Axel realized he wanted that, too. He did need to repair his reputation with the public. And possibly with himself.

Maddie was right. He was self-absorbed. His brother had called him conceited mere minutes ago. Axel wanted a different image, and he knew change would only come if he acted on that desire. He thought of Lynx's request and knew he had to give it serious consideration.

"My brother actually just asked me to volunteer at his school, filling in for an ill drama teacher." His heart pounded at the thought.

"That's brilliant! Right up your alley. It's authentic. Please tell me you said yes." Joni sounded enthusiastic. "I can send someone in to take a few pictures, and I know just the person to do a small write-up.

This is perfect timing. Why didn't you tell me when I first got on the call?"

Axel chuckled as Joni rambled on, already in planning mode. He interjected, "I'm not doing it to win over the public." Once he uttered the words, Axel recognized he spoke the truth. It wasn't about him. He wanted to help his brother, and Maddie had said she would help. That was good enough for him. "No press. No pictures."

"What?" Joni said. "You need this."

"I don't need anything but my family. My work will speak for itself. I can't live my life for my fans. I've got to live for me. For my family."

She changed tactics. "How about I try to spin the story and say that you planned a special surprise for Natasha and were caught off guard? Then you can take her to some exotic place—I'll arrange it—and you can post a few carefully planned pics on social media. Voilà!"

Her tenacity was why he had hired her, but Axel wasn't about to make any grand gestures he knew he didn't mean. He smiled and said, "No."

Joni sputtered. "I can't help you if you won't let me..."

"How about you use this time to focus on the fact that you're going to give birth soon and get your nursery set up—at my expense," he offered.

"I already did that," she shot back. "My baby is safe, protected, inside my uterus. You're not. I need to focus on you."

Axel remained silent.

"Fine. Ugh. Enjoy the drama class. Take pictures. We'll talk more in a week or two."

Axel knew she was going to come back with something else to try to change his mind. But he doubted he would. He sent Lynx a text telling him he would fill in for Ms. Millner. Lynx responded with a dancing GIF.

He would ask Maddie to get him a newer, modern script for *The Sound of Music*.

For the first time in a long time, Axel was doing something without a hidden benefit. He had nothing to gain from helping the kids, although he was scared by the thought of facing teenagers. But a part of him was excited. And it felt good.

Chapter Seven

Maddie was in her bathroom, hiding out, and that didn't feel good. She rested her head against the shower stall, her towel wrapped around her, and willed herself not to allow Axel's words to his publicist to affect her. But they had. And they hurt. She bit back a sob. This was the second time Axel had made her feel less than. No. She was allowing his thoughtless words to make her feel that way.

He had only spoken his truth. That he saw her as undatable. *No one would believe I'm dating Maddie. She not the type of woman I usually date...*

Harmless words that jabbed her heart, chipping at the wall of confidence she had painstakingly built around her. She knew she was a plain Jane. She had heard it enough from her mother and had almost buckled under the disappointment of not being good enough.

Maddie lifted her head. She hadn't buckled, though. She had homed in on her strengths. Her loyalty. Her kindness. Her work ethic. She knew Axel appreciated that, but he was too dismissive when it came to her feelings, her career, her worth. Maddie hadn't missed his lack of response when it came to *A Summer's Dream*. Maybe it was time she stopped trying to get him to do something he didn't want to do.

She was an independent, capable woman. A woman with a choice. She didn't have to work for someone who took her for granted or who dismissed her feelings. She would be thirty in a few weeks, and it was time for a change. Having Axel in her space was a great inconvenience. She had run errands, cleaned up after him, cooked... Maddie was his assistant, but what she was doing now was way beyond that. She was doing the job of a wife. And she didn't want to be his wife. She didn't want to be his anything.

Not anymore.

Maybe it was time she listened to Keri and Rochelle. Both had texted to say she had made a mistake by not going with them. What she needed to do was dump her pride and take her mother's advice. Faran had called her the day before to tell her about an internship opportunity. Her mother wanted to put in a recommendation, but Maddie told her mother to give her time to think about it.

Maddie finished drying off, applied a generous

amount of lotion and donned a sheer set of nude underwear. Then she went into her closet to search for
the orange romper she had purchased to wear on her
trip. The trip she hadn't gone on because of Axel.
How much of her life would he impact? Was this the
future she would be looking at, where her needs and
aspirations were secondary?

"Not going to happen," she muttered, as she
slipped into the romper and searched for a cardigan.
Next, she tamed her hair into a high bun—making
sure her edges were snatched—put on light makeup
and pushed her feet into a pair of canvas slip-ons fea-
turing an African woman with a basket on her head.
Compared to her other footwear, these were modest,
but Maddie wanted to be able to walk with ease so
she could get clarity. Cement her decision.

When she returned to the living area, Axel was
right where she'd left him, glued to his computer.
He gave her the once over and asked, "Going somewhere?"

"Yeah. I need some space," Maddie said.

"Space from me?"

She nodded.

He cocked his head. "What's going on?" His gentle tone made her feel guilty, but she shook off the
feeling.

"There's a condo for sale next door—two, actually. Either way, I need you to move out."

He scooted to the edge of the couch. "Did I do
something to offend you?" he asked and then pointed
to the screen. *Casablanca* still remained frozen, Hum-

phrey holding Ingrid in his arms. "About an hour ago, we were sharing, taking in the film. What changed?"

Maddie lowered her head to her chin and looked down at her feet. "I don't want to talk about it." She made herself meet his eyes. "Keri's coming home in a couple of days, and she shouldn't have to deal with you staying here."

He pinned her with a gaze. "I won't know what I did wrong if you don't tell me."

There was no way Maddie was going to admit his offhanded comments to Joni had stung. In fact, she doubted Axel would understand. Instead, she donned a cloak of anger, welcoming it like a blanket on a cold day. "This is my space, and I have the right not to give you an explanation." Her chin wobbled at the last word, and she cursed her weakness. She couldn't afford for Axel to cajole her into changing her mind.

However, his next words stunned her. "I do agree that it's time for me to leave. I'm sorry if I was an imposition." Axel stood and brushed some stray popcorn off his leg, and the kernels fell to the floor, rolling under the coffee table. "If you find me a place, I'll hire movers and a cleaning crew. In a day or two, it will be like I was never here."

His words punched her gut. Now she really had to get out of there. Here he was agreeing with her, and she had to fight the sudden urge to beg him to stay. Her emotions were on a seesaw, and she was not all right with that. With a quick nod, Maddie grabbed her house key and wallet and sailed through the door.

She stuffed her hands in her cardigan pockets and

walked down the stairs and to the parking lot, then stopped. She had no idea where she wanted to go. The light breeze outside soothed her, and she closed her eyes and inhaled. She had done the right thing asking Axel to leave. He was messing with her equilibrium, her well-being. His words to Joni had impacted her self-esteem with the force of a cannonball. Already, Maddie could breathe more easily not being in his presence. She inhaled and exhaled before spreading her arms, welcoming the feel of the sun on her face.

After checking the weather app and seeing that there was only a five percent chance of rain, Maddie decided to walk to the nearby park since the sun was out. A couple of runners were farther down the trail, but otherwise the park was empty, which suited her fine.

A memory of her walking this same trail with her Auntie Dawn made Maddie smile. Her father's sister, a music teacher, had been one of the most creative people Maddie had ever met. Her aunt had never married but had always been involved in the arts—singing and writing poetry—and had made many fascinating connections.

Auntie Dawn had lived in New York and performed on Broadway, putting Jamaica on the map, as Maddie's father would brag. Maddie had been enthralled with her aunt's stories and record collection. When she passed suddenly of an aneurysm, Maddie and her father had been devastated. She had inherited the condo, paid in full, and her father had taken the record collection.

Maddie strolled around the circumference of the park while she reminisced, but then her thoughts shifted to Axel. It was time she stopped waiting for him to take her seriously as a scriptwriter. Left to him, she would wait the rest of her life.

Her phone rang. Seeing it was her mother, Maddie decided to let the call go to voice mail. She would call Faran later and accept the internship position, if it was still available. For now, Maddie was enjoying her solitude.

A line of ducks waddled past her, with the mother duck leading the way. They were walking close to the edge of the pond. The last duck in line couldn't seem to keep up, tripping over its feet. But that didn't stop the duckling. It was scrappy and determined, straggling behind. Then, to Maddie's surprise, the little duck decided to leave the group and dip into the pond, swimming past the group, quacking as it went by.

Maddie laughed. "Go on," she said, admiring the bird's spirit. It had spunk.

Her mouth dropped open. She stopped. Chill bumps popped up on her arms. That little duck was her. She touched her chest. It was time. Time for her to go on her own path.

She hurried back to her condo and went to knock on Axel's—er, the door to her spare room. Axel called out for her to enter.

Standing by the door, Maddie squared her shoulders and began. "It's time I forge my own path. I'm tired of being the last duckling in line."

He frowned. "Huh? You're not making any sense

right now. What on earth are you trying to say?" Axel was looking at her like she was speaking another language, but Maddie would hold her position.

Lifting her chin, Maddie said, "You're right. That analogy won't make sense to anyone but me. So let me use two words I know you'll understand." She took a deep breath. "I quit." She exhaled.

Axel gasped, but she ignored him and pressed on.

"I'm handing in my resignation. Being the professional that I am, I am giving you ample time to find a replacement. Consider this my two weeks' notice."

After uttering the words, she inhaled, feeling a sense of relief and freedom. Like she had taken off a dress that was two sizes too small and could now breathe. And she should be able to, having just decided to unload 230 pounds of male off her small shoulders.

Lunging to his feet, Axel touched her forehead. "Are you serious? Or ill? Because you're not making sense right now. A fever would explain your incoherence."

"No. I'm just fine," she said, stepping back and fighting the urge to skip. Just saying the words had removed the invisible wedge in her chest. She even smiled.

"You can't quit on me like that for no reason," Axel ground out, his brows knitted together. "What do you want? A bigger car? More money? A house? A raise? Name your price. I'll call your bluff. Everyone has a price and, in your case, I'll pay it double— triple if I have to."

Maddie lost her smile. He actually thought this was some kind of stunt. This man did not know her at all. In a no-nonsense tone, she said, "I'm not bluffing. If I wanted a raise or more money, I would say so. And the fact that you would try to bribe me with material things means that you don't have a clue about the real me. I don't want anything you have to offer." She shrugged and mumbled, "Not anymore, anyways."

"But you promised you'd help me with the school play if I accepted." He shook his head. "I know this might surprise you, but I volunteered because I want to help. I took your words to heart and I texted Lynx. So, why would you bail on me now?"

Maddie brushed a small leaf off her cardigan, steeling herself against his pleading eyes, refusing to be ensnared by their deep brown depths. "I'm not bailing. I'm moving on. I intend to keep my word. For the next fourteen days, I will be right there with you by your side. But after that, you're on your own."

Chapter Eight

Twelve days.

That's all he had left with the best assistant he had ever had. And Axel had no clue why.

Axel and Maddie sat next to each other in the auditorium, watching the students perform a run-through of the musical, but there might as well have been a fifty-mile gulf separating them. He had tried to broach the topic of her departure, but all he had gotten were cool, polite responses.

Oh, she did her job well. Exceeded expectations. In two days, Maddie had found him a private, furnished mansion about twenty minutes from where she lived. She had stocked his refrigerator and pantry with his must-haves—including Cap'n Crunch—and ensured he had a wardrobe, weights and a Peloton bike. Then

Maddie had called the school district to fast-track his security clearance so he could enter the school building with the proper credentials. Axel's physical and temporary career needs were more than adequately met. There was nothing she hadn't thought of as his assistant. But as someone he saw as a friend, Maddie had no words for him.

He missed her.

Missed her humor, her ready smile, her quick wit.

Axel didn't like this matter-of-fact person who treated him like he was…her boss? If only he could figure out what he had done to get frozen out of Maddie's space, her life, he would be able to fix things. But when it came to him, those remarkable eyes remained impersonal.

And he hated it. It created a fire in his gut and Axel had to summon all his self-control not to snap or stir her temper. He needed every bit of these twelve days. He sighed. Feeling Maddie's eyes on him, Axel faced her with a ready smile. And got nothing.

That's it. He would ask again. "Maddie, are you going to tell me what's wrong?"

"There's nothing wrong," she returned in an irritating, saccharine tone now reserved for him. "I just know it's time for me to move on. Turning thirty makes you reevaluate your life."

One of the students got behind the piano, and began to sing, "Climb Ev'ry Mountain."

Wrinkling his nose, Axel searched his memory, and tried to tune out the nasally tone of the singer before him. The young lady began the chorus, and Axel gritted his teeth to keep from covering his ears. He had attended high school plays with some amazing student vocalists back when he was in high school. The standards must have changed, because the young lady was straining, and others had their hands over their mouths to hide their chuckles. Axel didn't stop her from singing, though. His mind was filled with Maddie.

Looking up at the ceiling as if it had answers, he wondered, had he forgotten Maddie's birthday? The exact date eluded him. But it would explain her anger. Giving her a gentle shove, "I'm sorry I forgot your birthday. Is that what this is about?" He stuffed a hand in his pocket, intending to pull out his wallet.

In a voice colder than an ice bath, she said, "You think I'm that shallow? This has nothing to do with you and everything to do with me." She pursed her lips. "To rephrase the lyrics from the oldie, 'I bet you think my life is about you.' Don't you?"

He rolled his eyes and faced forward, removing his hand from his pocket. So, he hadn't missed her birthday... He had enough experience with women to know he should not provide an answer to that question or give her his credit card. "I don't know what to do to get things back to the way they were before."

"Let me put your mind at ease," she whispered. "There's nothing you can do. So don't waste your time trying." Then, pointing toward the stage, she said, "If I were you, I would center my attention on the students who are doing their best to impress you."

Unable to tolerate the off-pitch tone of the student

any longer, Axel stood and held up a hand, shouting, "Cut. End scene," so he could be heard over her singing, if one could call it that. He cleared his throat. "Good effort." The pianist ended with a clang. The rest of the students onstage huddled together.

The young lady twisted her hands. "My allergies are acting up." Her cheeks were pink with embarrassment and her eyes filled. Axel walked up to the stage, pretending not to notice that the teens were starstruck.

Maddie rushed past him and went to hug the girl. "It's all right, sweetheart. Take some elderberry and vitamin C. Your voice will be back in no time." Cocking her head, she asked the girl's name. Axel envied how gentle Maddie was being with her.

"Lizzie," she croaked out, her lips chapped from her braces.

The other performers snickered. Axel chided them, "You're not just a troupe—you're a family. This is your drama family. Would you be laughing if this were your sister or your brother standing here?"

A few tucked their chins to their chests, looking embarrassed.

Axel directed his attention on the young boy playing Captain Von Trapp, who kept his shoulders squared, and didn't appear the least bit apologetic. The youth, who said his name was Jeff, had a cloak of arrogance, and defiance shot from his eyes, reminding Axel of himself at that age.

Placing his hands behind his back, Axel stalked away a few feet before whipping around, assuming the character of Captain Von Trapp. He puffed his chest and made his way over to where Maddie stood, walking with the smooth ease that Christopher Plummer had when he played the role.

The teens gasped before straightening. Circling around the teens, he mimicked Captain Von Trapp addressing his children. Some giggled, but they all played along.

Taking Maddie's hand, hoping she would play along as Maria, Axel snatched her close, wrapping his arms around her and ad-libbed, "Somewhere in my youth or childhood..."

Her breath shaky, Maddie finished, "I must have done something good." Her chin lifted and her eyes shone behind those glasses, her chest heaving against his. He had never held Maddie like this, and the scent of citrus from her hair teased his nostrils.

Axel felt a slice through his heart. His body hummed with electricity and something else he couldn't identify. His mind registered her plump, kissable lips, and he had a compelling need to press his lips against hers. Get a taste. But no. He was acting out a scene. Axel dragged himself out of her arms—and out of character.

For several tense seconds, Axel met her gaze, his eyes taking in the reddish tint of her cheeks. Maddie placed her hands over her lips before she scampered off the stage to sit in the front row.

The students broke into spontaneous applause. They must have thought they were still acting, but Axel knew different. The moment between them had been very real...and confusing.

Feeling about a dozen pairs of eyes on him, Axel addressed the group. "It's not enough to have talent," he said. "You have to be believable, and that comes when you're in touch with a person, when you know them—" He pivoted until he faced Maddie and said in a low, entreating voice, "When they are family. And family does not betray family."

Once again, it was Axel and Maddie. She fiddled with her blouse, refusing to acknowledge his words. His accusation.

He faced the students and continued, "To make this performance epic, you have to support each other."

The young man went over and squeezed Lizzie's shoulders. Then the other performers surrounded her, whispering words of support and encouragement. Axel's lips curved into a smile. Wiping his brow, he dared to look Maddie's way once again.

Even from where he stood, he could see her eyes glistened. She gave him a soft smile and a thumbs-up. He preened under her admiration. Then he directed them to run the scene again, telling Lizzie to rest her voice. He advised that if someone forgot their lines, someone would jump in to cover.

Before they began, Maddie returned to the stage to help prep the scene props. She ran them through a few transitions, which helped the students navigate the props better.

Then the students performed the scene again, much better than they had done before. They moved with an energy, helping each other through the final act. Maddie praised them, clapping her hands. Axel held back his praise, though equally proud.

The sudden bang of the auditorium door broke the mood. His brother Lynx raced down the aisle. "Sorry I wasn't able to greet you. I had a parent conference." Lynx's long legs covered the distance, and he jogged up the steps. The brothers embraced, and Lynx patted Axel on the back. "Thank you so much for doing this. I can't tell you how much we appreciate having you here."

Axel nodded. "I'm enjoying it so far." With a start, he realized he spoke the truth. And he attributed that to Maddie.

Lynx went to speak to each student, and Axel leaned against the piano and observed, impressed with how his brother treated each child with respect. He cared about them, asking about their family members or their classwork. The students looked at Lynx with awe, and it was easy to see the respect was mutual.

Axel felt a pang. That's what he wanted in his personal and professional life—respect, not starstruck hero worship. Natasha hadn't respected that he wasn't ready for marriage. If she had, she wouldn't have proposed. But, if she hadn't, Axel wouldn't be here. He wouldn't have experienced the thrill he had felt with Maddie in his arms, and he wouldn't have a renewed desire to reinvent himself as an actor.

The few minutes he had played the role of the navy captain had made him come alive, feeding his need for a role that would challenge him, take his career on a path with deeper meaning. He would call Ralph to scout for more scripts and renew his search for the right one.

As for Maddie, Axel eyed her as she continued to interact with the students. She had a charm that drew them in. *She will make a great mother one day*, he thought.

Wait. Why was he hyper tuned in to Maddie? Why had he had that reaction when she was in his arms? Maybe it was because she was leaving… Yes, that had to be it. He was in a state of panic over her departure less than two weeks from now.

Maybe instead of fighting it, he needed to respect her decision. Give her the same respect she extended to him and others. His stomach clenched. His throat tightened. Maddie was ready to set sail, experience new paths, and he had a choice to make—support her or stand in her way. Either way, Axel would lose her as his assistant.

Unless…he gave her something she wanted more than leaving. Like agreeing to take the lead in her screenplay.

He rushed to Maddie and pulled her to the side, delivering his news, expecting to see her face brighten.

She raised a brow, eyes filled with wary suspicion and daresay a little hope. "Have you read the script?" she asked.

Axel shook his head. "No. Not yet."

"Then how can you commit when you haven't read it? How do you know it's any good?"

"I don't," he was forced to admit.

Maddie shook her head. "I should have known. This is all about you getting your way. I'm going to start interviewing for my replacement. The minute I find someone, I'm leaving."

He opened his mouth to say he was going to read her script that night. But Maddie held up a hand. "Save the empty promises, Axel. We both know that underneath that hot body and sexy smile of yours is nothing but…a flake. A fraud. You're nobody's hero. Least of all mine."

Chapter Nine

"Wow. He is fine," Keri said, blowing out a low whistle and eyeing the server who had seated them and taken their orders. The women had met up for dinner at Cheddar's once Maddie sent Keri an SOS text.

Her friends had returned from their vacation the night before and Keri was flying out again that night to Mexico, so it was a good time for them to connect and catch up. Rolling her eyes, Maddie asked Keri about her vacation.

"Girl, it was off the chain. Especially once Axel hooked us up." Keri pulled out her phone and shared pictures and videos—ones she hadn't posted on social media. "Rochelle met a young man, and let's just say that Stella got her groove back."

Cracking up, Maddie shook her head. "Rochelle is a hot mess. She needs to leave those young boys alone."

Lifting a brow, Keri said, "Don't knock it till you try it. Those young men are *strong*, if you get my drift." She rocked her hips suggestively. "They've got stamina."

"I can't with the both of you," Maddie said with a chuckle, her tone nonjudgmental. "We're not that old. You don't have to go robbing the cradle."

"Hey, life is about living, and I'm living it." Keri raised her hands in the air. "As long as they eighteen, they legal."

"What about you?" Maddie asked. "Did you meet anyone?"

Keri shook her head, growing serious. "No, I was there to relax. I read and I shopped. And I kept Rochelle out of trouble."

Maddie nodded but reached over to cover her friend's hand with her own. After her breakup the prior year, Keri hadn't dated, and she still wasn't interested in dating. She was all about self-love.

"I'm glad to know you didn't rebound into another relationship and that you're taking the time to heal," Maddie said, giving Keri's hand a light squeeze. "That's important."

"My therapist suggested it, and I'm glad I took her advice." Keri lifted her shoulders. "I don't think I'll ever put myself out there again. I'm not handing my heart over to anyone again, giving a hundred percent and getting nothing in return." Her voice held a slight edge of bitterness.

"He wasn't the one," Maddie insisted. "So don't close yourself off."

Keri played with the rings on her finger and shifted the conversation. "Speaking of closing yourself off, what's going on with you?"

Their food orders arrived. Both women thanked the server, waiting until he had left before going back to their conversation.

Maddie squared her shoulders and spewed her discontent. She filled Keri in on her resignation and her conversation with Axel, along with her parting words.

Keri's eyes went wide. "Whoa. That was harsh."

Maddie swallowed a spoonful of her hearty baked potato soup, her regret spoiling the taste of one of her favorite comfort foods. "I did text him an apology, but he hasn't responded," she said.

Her chest squeezed. The minute the words flew out her mouth, Maddie had wanted to snatch them back. Axel had looked crushed, which hadn't been her intention. In fact, he had grounds to fire her. But instead of apologizing, Maddie had rushed out of the auditorium, choking back her tears.

Maddie pushed her bowl to the middle of the small table, knowing she wouldn't be able to eat any more. She had also ordered the salmon Caesar pasta salad but knew she would have to have her server box up her food.

Keri stuck her spoon into her chicken pot pie and scooped out a generous portion before using her finger to keep the contents from spilling over. Putting it into her mouth, Keri closed her eyes and groaned. "This is *so* good."

"I don't even know how you eat so much and don't gain any weight," Maddie said, shaking her head. If she ate even one half of what Keri consumed, she would have to work out for hours every day.

"It's all genetics," Keri said with a shrug. "My mother is the same way. And if you think I can eat, you should see her go at it."

Keri's words made Maddie think of Faran. Maddie had not inherited her mother's metabolism or personality. She waited for the usual pinch of sadness, but none came. She must have grown into her own skin, so to speak. Yes, Maddie loved herself. What she pined for was acceptance. Being worthy in her mother's eyes. Good enough. Taking the internship her mother offered would do that...

Waving a hand, Keri joked, "Earth to Maddie. Check in, Maddie. Check in."

"Huh?" she said. "Did you say something?"

Keri twirled her fork in Maddie's direction. "I asked what was on your mind but you zoned out on me."

"I was thinking about this internship I heard about," Maddie said, squeezing a tiny section of the tablecloth between her index finger and thumb.

Her friend leaned in, shifting her food to the side. "What internship? Have you been holding out on me?"

"Relax. I only heard about it a couple days ago, and I was still processing if I wanted to go. It's actually a paid internship."

Keri gestured for Maddie to explain.

Maddie cleared her throat. "Someone I know has a connection to Artie Rae."

Keri gasped, her eyes going wide. "Artie Rae? The award-winning director? Wow. I'm impressed."

"Yeah. Well, he's looking for a directorial assistant for a science fiction love story that's supposed to be the next *Lake House* or something. Right now, they're securing the cast and building the set, but Artie wants to start filming soon. It's set in Oregon, so I'd have to relocate for a few months."

"What's there to think about?" Keri asked, her eyes flashing with excitement. "This is a no-brainer. You've got to go for this. Especially if you have an in. Working with Artie Rae would put you in the big leagues. You need to grab this with both hands and don't look back."

"Yes…you're right. I guess…"

"Listen, you know I'm right." Her eyes narrowed. "I don't get the hesitation. Unless…" She went quiet.

"Unless what?"

Keri cocked her head and asked in a gentle voice, "Do you have feelings for Axel? Feelings above and beyond naturally caring about someone?"

"What?" Maddie reared back in her seat. "No. Why would you ask me that? Axel has absolutely nothing to do with my hesitation. I just got done saying that I gave him my two weeks' notice, so what you're asking makes no sense." Neither did her sudden racing heart and clammy hands, but Maddie would ignore that.

"No. Your reaction makes no sense," Keri shot back, pointing her index finger Maddie's way. "You're being handed the chance of a lifetime on a platter, and you're filled with indecision. Makes me wonder why."

In a flash, Maddie recalled how it had felt taking on the role of Maria from *Sound of Music* and being in Axel's arms, close to his chest, drawing his energy. He had been acting, assuming a part, but Maddie had felt a very real reaction. A tingle. A surge of electrical impulses humming everywhere their bodies had made contact. She had been thrilled, scared, intrigued. That knowledge had her cutting contact, and yes, she had run, busying herself with helping the teens, feeling exposed at her sudden...attraction.

No.

She wasn't attracted to Axel. She wouldn't join the hype or get caught up. Besides, her indecision had nothing to do with Axel and everything to do with her mother. Accepting the internship would be taking a handout instead of earning her way. Giving herself a mental shake, Maddie faced Keri, whose eyes had narrowed with suspicion.

"This isn't about Axel. I just don't feel right using my connection to get the job instead of going through the regular channels."

Raising her voice, Keri asked, "Why not? People do that all the time. It's called helping."

"But I'd always be questioning if I got the job because of who I know versus my skills."

"Girl, please. Hollywood is all about who you know. Most of the major actors had parents or grandparents in the business. They all got a leg up to get where they are now."

"Not all," Maddie persisted. "There are plenty tales of rags to riches. Even Axel made it on his own merit."

Keri scoffed. "That's overrated. They would have been glad to get a hookup. You're overthinking this, as usual. Your connection might get you through the door, but it's your work ethic, your skills, your talent that will help you keep it. You've been praying for a chance, so why say no when this might be your answer?"

Keri was right, and Maddie told her so. After settling the bill and gathering her personal items and takeout, Maddie sat behind the steering wheel of her car and reflected on Keri's words. She could admit that her major hindrance to her success was herself. Her pride. She didn't want Faran lording it over her that she had gotten Maddie a job. She didn't want to be in Faran's shadow. She wanted her career to be about her personal achievement and nothing to do with Artie wanting an in with her mom.

Faran dabbled in acting, and Artie had reached out, wanting Faran to play the mother of the heroine. That's how her mother had heard about the internship. So, Maddie was practically guaranteed the position. But then everybody would know she was Faran's daughter. She couldn't and wouldn't deny her mother on set. That would be cruel, and Faran would be hurt. Her mother might be disappointed that she hadn't created a supermodel offspring, but Faran was proud of Maddie, bragging about her daughter's accomplishments in every conversation. Deep down, Maddie knew her mother loved her, wanted to help her. There was nothing wrong with that.

It was Maddie who had the problem.

It was Maddie who couldn't escape the long reach of her mother's spotlight.

She recalled it all. Shrinking away from the questioning eyes and furrowed brows traveling up her frame, wondering about her true relation. Enduring the speculative glances and whispers about whether or not she was adopted. Gritting her teeth at the fake smiles of those who thought they could use Maddie to get to her mother.

Maddie rubbed her eyes, folded her arms across the steering wheel and then rested her head on them. Ugh, it was all too much. In twelve days, she was out of a job. Dangled before her was a career-making opportunity, so there was no question about what she needed to do.

She sighed. So why was she hesitating?

In a word, Axel.

She didn't want to leave. Wasn't ready to leave him.

His magnetism was intoxicating, his arms powerful and strong.

That knowledge gave her a jolt, caused her stomach to swirl. *Jeez, Maddie. Stop thinking about it. It was a quick scene. A few seconds in his arms.* Yet, here she was, replaying that moment over and over like it was a hot new summer jam. Like she was one of his groupies. No. No. She wouldn't let that happen. She wouldn't be one of them. She hadn't for the past couple years, so why was she letting him get to her now?

Maddie started up her car and sped back to her condo. Driving as if she could outrun her thoughts.

But they wouldn't rest.

The question Keri had asked inside Cheddar's haunted her. She cared about Axel. But she wouldn't say her feelings were above and beyond. They had maybe…intensified because of her impending departure. Yes, that's it. Her heightened emotions were understandable.

No. She needed to be honest with herself. This wasn't about emotions. It was attraction. Plain and simple.

Just a normal everyday girl attracted to a sexier-than-should-be-allowed man. She snorted. If only it were that simple. She pulled into an empty spot in front of her complex. Just as she put the gear in Park, her cell pinged.

Maddie dug in her bag and pulled out her cell phone. Her heart thumped when she saw the text from Axel. Her eyes scanned the contents.

Sorry. Just seeing this. I'm at the hospital. It's my mom. Everybody's here…

Maddie gasped. Tanya Harrington was one of the fittest, strongest people she knew. She wanted to call Axel but knew he would have called if he could or were up to it. She also knew he needed her there. The ellipsis at the end of his message was his silent plea for her presence. She knew that. So she fired off a text.

I'm on my way.

After rereading his text, her heart began to pound in her chest. Worry over Tanya and Axel writhed in her stomach like a restless toddler fighting sleep. She had to get to the Love Creek hospital—the only one in town—but first, she would stop at the nearby Chipotle. Maddie was sure they hadn't eaten.

She tossed her phone on the passenger seat and rushed out of the lot.

Chapter Ten

Axel held his breath and counted to ten before making eye contact with the man huddled in the corner of the room. Axel's designer shades and baseball cap were a poor disguise, but he had only been concerned with his mother's health once Lynx had rushed back into the auditorium to give him the news that Tanya had passed out. Axel had ridden over with Lynx and tried not to attract attention, to keep a low profile, but of course he had been spotted.

And then followed.

The nurses had led them to this small waiting area while his mother was being seen. Ralph had emailed Axel a couple scripts to look over, and he had welcomed the distraction. He had tried to focus on the words on his screen instead of the interloper across from him, but Axel wanted him gone.

Dressed in a trench coat and a fedora hat, the man hunkered down into the chair and glanced away.

Most of the people in Love Creek knew him and weren't impressed with his fame, so this man was most likely an outsider. An opportunist. *Paparazzi.*

The man shifted his position and once again looked over to where Axel was seated. Four of his brothers sat in different corners of the room, waiting on word of their mom. Hawk was on his way from Miami, having just returned from a game in Denver, and Brigg, a police officer, would head over as soon as he secured a replacement for his shift. Axel's father was in the back with his mother.

Drake and Ethan came close and flanked him. His silent guards. A former Olympian turned swim coach, Ethan wore swim trunks and a T-shirt. Drake was dressed in a polo shirt and slacks, typical wear in his job as a middle school counselor.

"Don't let him get to you," Drake whispered under his breath.

"Yeah, bro," Ethan said, "Remain cool."

Axel made eye contact with Lynx, who had his arm around his fiancée, Shanna Jacobs. Shanna gave him a thumbs-up and a quick smile before snuggling closer to Lynx. Watching them made Axel think of Maddie, for some reason. He hadn't extended an invitation, but he hoped his assistant—now for less than two weeks longer—would show up. He could use her calm stability. She would know the right words to temper the raging anxiety in his stomach. Because he was freaking out. His insides raged, and if he wasn't under surveillance, Axel would be pacing the room.

The man got up and came to sit across from Axel. Like an eel, he slithered close, waiting for Axel to show a reaction. And to get news about his mother.

Axel swallowed his burgeoning fury and pulled the cap lower. This was a family emergency. Yet all this man saw was dollar signs—the chance to have breaking news splashed across a cheesy mag. *The man's bold*, Axel thought.

Caleb stood and walked over to stand in front of the interloper. "You shouldn't be here."

"I'm waiting on someone and I have every right to be here," the man croaked out.

"I don't care about your rights," Caleb said. "See your way out."

"I'm not going anywhere," he challenged, jumping to his feet.

Axel stood. "Get out."

"Make me."

His brothers shot to their feet and pushed Axel out of the way.

"Don't do anything rash," Ethan warned.

"I'll go get security," Drake said and rushed out of the room.

"You enjoy being a nuisance?" Axel yelled.

"I have no idea what you're talking about," the intruder said, though his eyes darted back and forth between the brothers, his fear evident. None of his brothers would touch him, though. They knew that to do so would make things worse for Axel. But Axel didn't care about his reputation. He needed an outlet for his worry, and this man was asking for it.

Axel bunched his fists.

"What is going on here?" a voice said from behind him.

A voice he knew well. A voice that brought him relief.

He uncurled his fingers and cocked his head. *Maddie*. She had come. His brothers backed off, and Axel released a huge breath.

Maddie held a couple of large bags in her hands. The aroma from the food made Axel's stomach growl. It had been about seven hours since he had eaten, two of which had been spent here in the emergency room. Ethan rushed to take the bags out of Maddie's hands.

"Maddie, you're an angel," Lynx said. "Shanna and I were just talking about getting takeout for everyone. Thanks so much."

"It's on Axel's dime, so I guess you need to be thanking him," she said, looking everywhere but at Lynx. Axel shook his head. Maddie had trouble accepting praise or being the center of everyone's focus. She always found a way to deflect.

His other brothers chimed in with more words of gratitude, filling Maddie in on the cause of dissension, as they unloaded the bags on a desk pushed against a wall in the room.

Glaring at the meddler, Maddie grabbed his arm and tugged. "Come with me." She led the man over to the entrance and whispered a few words. They had a rapid conversation before he gave a small nod, handed her a card and scurried out of the room.

Knitting his brows, Axel walked over to where she stood and asked, "What did you say to him?"

She shrugged. "I promised Scott an exclusive if he respected your need for privacy now."

"You're on a first-name basis with that clown? You shouldn't have done that. Those people are slime," Axel said through gritted teeth. Behind him, he could hear his brothers helping themselves to the food.

"Well, it was the best I could do, and if he doesn't get the story, someone else will. At least with him, we can control what gets posted. You know that."

He knew she was right. He had a love-hate relationship with the media. If they stopped taking his picture, then he wouldn't be as relevant, as in demand. He wouldn't be able to command a seven-figure salary for his movies. But their angling to take his picture, to splatter his face on their papers, was also a personal intrusion.

"I still don't like it," he fussed.

Rolling her eyes, Maddie said, "Get over it. At least now you can focus fully on your mother. I saw Drake when I was coming in, and he said your mother passed out." She walked over to the food and picked up a plate. "What do you want?"

"You know what I like," Axel said. "Thank you. I don't know if I'll be able to eat, though."

"You need to," she said, her tone signifying she wasn't going to take no for an answer. She proceeded to add brown rice, black beans, veggies, salsa and chicken to his plate. "I didn't know what to get, so I got a little bit of everything—well, a lot, actually." She asked in a gentle tone, "Has there been any word on Tanya?"

"Not yet. My dad's back there with her, but we haven't had an update."

The door opened, and Axel swung around to see if it was his father. It was Drake returning, without security in tow, but with Brigg on his heels.

"We saw that joker on our way back," Drake supplied. "Security is seeing him out the door, but he didn't put up a fuss once he saw one of Love Creek's finest here," he said, pointing a finger at Brigg.

Brigg shrugged, then made a beeline toward the food.

Maddie handed Axel his plate and then reached for another plate to get some food for herself. She didn't take too much. Once she was finished, they grabbed silverware, and Axel led Maddie to a couple of chairs near the corner of the room.

"I'm so glad you're here," he said, dipping his fork into his food.

"You knew I would come," she said, not touching her meal. She chewed on her lower lip and drew a deep breath before looking him square in the eyes.

Axel lifted a hand, knowing what she was going to say. "You don't have to say anything. I did see your apology."

Shaking her head, Maddie wouldn't be deterred. "No, I shouldn't have used those words. I—I don't even know why I said them. It was mean, and that's not me at all. I was afraid you were going to fire me, even though I already quit. So, I was relieved when I saw your text come through." She waved a hand. "Not at the circumstances, but at the fact that you were still talking to me. You're infuriating, but I...I won't try to excuse my actions." She appeared to struggle to find her next words before she exhaled. "I'm sorry. That's what it comes down to."

A lock of her hair fell across her face, resting across her nose. Maddie blew on the errant curl. Axel placed a spoonful of food in his mouth before using the back of his hand to move it out of her face. That simple act caused an instant reaction with him. A heart pull. The why wasn't something he was ready to explore.

"Look, we're all good. If I'm being honest, there's some truth to your words. To Natasha and the rest of the world, I'm a flake. I knew she wanted more, and I should have ended things instead of stringing her along." He looked away and focused on the painting behind her head. "And I am a fraud. I keep taking these roles I know I don't want because I'm afraid."

"Then put yourself out there," Maddie said, snapping his attention back to her earnest face. "I believe in you. You have mad talent, and your skills are off the charts. You're at the place where you can do whatever you want. Take a chance. What are you afraid of?"

"Failing. Sucking." He shoveled more food in his mouth after that confession.

"That's not a good enough reason not to try." She

placed her plate on the small table. Most of her food had remained untouched. She must not be hungry. "Even if it's a flop, you will have learned something. You would have grown."

Cocking his head, Axel asked, "How do you know that?"

She shifted her body before looking down at her hands. "You're not the only celebrity I'm close to."

After that cryptic comment, Axel scooted close. He didn't remember seeing another name on her résumé. In fact, she hadn't had much experience when he had hired her. But before he could ask, his father entered the room.

Everyone gathered around Patrick for news.

"How's Mom?" Brigg asked, his hand on his holster.

Hawk walked in and rushed over to join the huddle. "What's going on? Can I see Mom?"

"Wait in line," Axel said, jutting his jaw. Hawk was the oldest of the brothers and seemed to think he had the right to everything first.

"Yeah," Drake said, giving him a shove.

"She's good. She's good," Patrick said, holding up a hand. The quiet authority in his tone made all the brothers go quiet. "The doctors are going to do an MRI to see if your mother had a stroke or seizure, but they have already ruled out a cardiac event."

Axel released a breath he hadn't realized he had been holding while his brothers bickered. His mother was strong and fit and the glue for the Harrington family. Before she married Patrick, it had been just the two of them. Axel and Tanya. A single mother finding her way after his father had jumped on a Greyhound, leaving Love Creek behind. Tanya was his rock and biggest supporter. He didn't want to think of a life without her.

"Do you think it was a panic attack?" Caleb asked.

Giving him a shove, Brigg said, "Dude, that makes no sense."

"You'd be surprised," Caleb returned, sounding like he knew what he was talking about. Axel frowned. He was going to have to reach out to his brother and press for more info. Caleb worked for the Love Creek School District as an attorney. His brother was always reading, studying. He didn't take breaks. Axel's and Hawk's eyes met, and Hawk nodded. Axel could see they were on the same page. Caleb needed a break, and they would give it to him.

But first—their mother.

"When can I see her?" Axel asked. "I want to see Mom for myself."

"We all want to see her," Ethan chimed in, giving Axel a cutting glance.

"Soon," Patrick promised, going over to peek into the containers of food. Shanna rushed over and commanded that their father sit, get off his feet. Then Lynx went to get their dad some food.

Axel watched the entire scene, disquieted. Today was the first time he was seeing his parents through a different lens. They were getting older. In fact, his father's last day of work was at the end of the month, before Thanksgiving break. They were planning him a great send-off.

He felt a hand curl around his, which startled him. Maddie had put her hand in his. It was comforting. Soothing. He tightened his grip, careful not to hurt her but grateful once again for her strength.

When he had sent the text, Axel hadn't been sure she would show up, as mad as she had been with him. Well, she had sounded disillusioned and disappointed, and knowing that had crushed him. Made him feel less than. He didn't want Maddie to see him in a negative light. Yet even feeling as she did, she was here standing next to him.

Supporting.

He wished she would take something in return. He'd offer her a car. A house. More money. But she wasn't interested. In fact, she had been angry. The only thing she had asked was for him to read her script...

A script he had promised to read several times. Yet he hadn't. He hadn't listened. He hadn't even read the first page. Shame filled him. Maddie was right. He was a flake.

Why hadn't he, though? Was it because he was afraid it was going to be good? Real good. Good enough to propel her career...and take her away? From him.

The truth cemented his feet and curdled his stomach. He really was selfish. Beyond words. He peered Maddie's way. His trying to hold on to her had only led to her giving him her two weeks' notice. He rubbed his chin with his free hand. Maybe the answer wasn't to try to keep her tied to him—not that he could, anyway. Maybe the answer was to help her find her path. Help her achieve her goals.

Yes, that was what he needed to do.

That's what he would do. For real this time.

Chapter Eleven

It was after midnight when Maddie entered her condo. Axel had insisted on driving her home, taking her car. He would return for her the next morning and they would travel to the high school together.

Thankfully, Tanya had been diagnosed with vertigo and discharged. His mother would be on bed rest for a few days and wasn't permitted to drive, but Maddie knew that wouldn't be an issue with all Tanya's sons ready to step in as chauffeurs.

The men had almost suffocated the much smaller woman with bear hugs, plying her with questions. Watching Tanya interact with her children made Maddie think of her mother. Faran was in great health, but she was alone in another country. Maddie considered the numerous times she'd evaded her mother's phone calls and texts. That didn't sit well with her. She looked at her watch. It was close to five thirty in the morning in Paris, but Maddie decided to give her mother a call.

"What's wrong?" Faran answered, sounding slightly panicked and like she had just awakened.

Guilt whipped at Maddie for waking her mother out of her sleep. "Nothing. Nothing, Mom. I just wanted to check on you. See how you're doing."

"Whew. The sun isn't even up yet," Faran said. "You had me thinking something happened to you."

"I'm sorry, Mom." Maddie swallowed. "I just… missed you."

"Oh, sweetheart. I miss you, too." Faran sounded more alert. "If you take that internship, we will get to see each other. For several months. I'm looking forward to that."

Cradling the phone close to her ear, Maddie searched her bag for her AirPods. "It would be good to spend time with you. Although I don't know how much quality time we would have when we both would be working." She found the little case and pulled out the buds.

"Please. We can find the time. That is, if you're willing to claim me as your mom." Faran snorted, though Maddie could hear the hurt in her voice.

"You know about that?" Maddie asked, wide-eyed, sticking her AirPods in her ears.

"Yes. Of course I know. A mother knows her child…" Faran trailed off. "But I'm still Mom. I'll still nag, reach out, make sure my flesh and blood, my one little lamb, is okay."

"I—I didn't think…"

"It's all right. I get it. I understand. You didn't ask to be born to a supermodel mom with the million-dollar face," Faran said, poking fun at her brand. "And you definitely didn't ask to be compared to me. I didn't want that for you. Why do you think I made sure you spent some of your summers in Love Creek with your auntie Dawn or with your father in Jamaica? I knew they could give you doses of the normal I couldn't. They could foster your psyche, keep you grounded in what matters."

Maddie's heart squeezed. Her mother knew more than she realized. She traipsed into her bedroom to get undressed.

Faran cleared her throat and continued. "While I have your ear, I just want to say I think you're extraordinary, and I'm proud of you. I know this was years ago, but I'm sorry you walked in hearing me call you ordinary and for the times I called you a plain Jane. I didn't mean it the way you think…"

"Mom, you don't have to apologize." Maddie's heart hammered. She regretted acting on the impulse to call. Her mother was tearing open old wounds like they were a bag of peanut M&Ms.

"No. Let me. Please," Faran pleaded. "You've never given me a chance to explain."

"I don't—"

"This life is a roller coaster. A lot of models I know end up on drugs or battling bulimia. I was nineteen when I got pregnant with you, and I didn't have a clue how to be a mother. I had a summer fling with a handsome man in Jamaica. Well, it was supposed to be fun. Your father wanted me to give you up so he and his wife could raise you, give you a normal life. She couldn't have children. But I wasn't having it."

Dropping her bag on the floor in her bedroom, Maddie allowed her mother to talk. She had never heard this side to the story before. Oh, she knew about her mother's affair with Paul Henry, a soon-to-be-married man. In fact, it had been the night before his wedding, but she hadn't known about her daddy asking Faran to give Maddie to him to raise.

"But though I kept you, I was worried. I was worried about this fast-paced, globe-trotting lifestyle. But my love superseded my worry. Motherhood was a scary, great experience. I wanted you to have an ordinary life, even though you had nannies and tutors while we traveled the world like nomads. I was glad—and a little jealous, actually—at how normal you were. How I managed to end up with an ordinary, grounded, caring daughter, I will never know. I may have used the wrong words, but I meant them in the best possible light."

Swallowing back tears, Maddie said, "Oh. I had no idea. I thought you were disappointed in me."

She heard sniffles through the phone. "Never disappointed. Not once. So, my recommending you for that internship isn't about doing you a favor, although every parent wants to help their child. It's about my acknowledging your greatness, your potential. I wouldn't recommend you if I didn't think you had the chutzpah to get it done."

"Wow." Tears pooled in Maddie's eyes and flowed down her cheeks. Now she was glad she had called her mother at this crazy hour. Faran was unguarded, honest. Her words, a truth serum, injected courage into Maddie's heart. The courage she needed to accept that internship position. "I'm going to call Artie tomorrow. I can't wait to work with you."

"Great," Faran exclaimed. "I can't wait to brag on you to everyone. I'm going to be your biggest fan, your hype woman, cheering you on."

"I hope I make you proud," Maddie said, slipping into her pajamas.

"I don't have to hope for what I already know."

Faran yawned and ended the call, saying she still needed three hours' worth of beauty sleep before she had to make an appearance at a fashion show.

Maddie got off the phone and headed to bed, but she didn't sleep much, thinking on her mother's words. She was all about believing in herself, but it felt good to have others believe in her as well. Especially her mom. Maddie knew she was going to need Faran those first few days without Axel.

The thought of leaving him terrified her.

But she knew she would. She must.

She had to embrace the new chapter, even if she didn't know how the scene would play out.

Anticipation blended with anxiety. Maddie tossed and turned most of the night, replaying her mother's words, wishing she had hit Record. Such high praise from her mother was rare but heartfelt. Close to day-break, Maddie decided to answer her body's plea and use the bathroom.

She slipped out of bed and made her way through the darkness, her foot encountering an unexpected obstacle. She tripped. Her ankle twisted, and Maddie fell hard, yelping in pain. She'd forgotten she had left her bag on the floor. Her foot throbbed. Maddie didn't want to stand on it, fearing it could be broken. She had to get to the hospital. Then she remembered that Axel had driven home with her car. Clutching her foot, Maddie scooted to the nightstand, where her phone was charging. She called Axel and tried to straighten her foot.

"Help me," she cried out.

"What happened?" Axel yelled.

Sharp pain sliced through her foot, and she had to fight back the tears. "Come quick. I think I broke my ankle."

"I'll be right there," he said, sounding frantic. "Don't go anywhere. I'm on my way."

"Where do you expect me to go?" Maddie shouted. "Of course I'm not going anywhere. Hurry up."

"Okay, sweetheart. I'm going through the door." Axel disconnected the call.

Maddie's eyes glazed over in pain. If she had been thinking straight, she would have called 9-1-1. She would have registered that Axel had called her *sweetheart* and she would have dissected those words, wondering why.

But none of that sank in as she hollered in pain.

Chapter Twelve

Obstinate. That's the word he would use to describe his assistant, because Maddie was trying his patience. They'd finally left the emergency room that morning after Maddie had been diagnosed with a mild sprain. The doctor had told her to ice her foot and keep it elevated. If necessary, she could use a light brace to ease the tension in her ankle.

Even though that had been their second trip to the ER in a matter of hours and it was now a few minutes after 9:00 a.m., Maddie had wanted to go to the high school, not wanting to disappoint the drama students. Axel had purchased doughnuts and bagels for breakfast, but instead of eating, they sat in the hospital parking lot arguing.

"I'm sure they'll understand," he had insisted before calling Lynx to let his brother know what had happened. Of course, Lynx had assured them he would find coverage. It was only then that Maddie had allowed him to take her home.

Then she protested when she realized Axel wasn't going back to her condo.

"Will you allow me to take care of you for once?" Axel shouted, trying to control his temper.

"Fine," she said, folding her arms. She didn't utter another word. Not one word when he scooped her into his arms and marched into the house, taking her to his bedroom. Both her brows shot up to her forehead, but she didn't say another word.

Which made him relieved...and suspicious.

His suspicions were confirmed when Maddie called on him every five minutes to turn on the television, fetch the remote, change the channel, get her water, get her fruit, fluff her pillows and change the channel yet again. Axel knew she was doing all that to get under his skin. She wanted him to lash out, to shout that there was nothing wrong with her hands, pack her up and take her home. However, that wasn't going to happen. He hid a chuckle. Her mission would be an epic fail.

What she failed to recollect was that Axel had six brothers who were masters at being annoying nuisances.

None were as cute as Maddie.

He had to admit that the more she tried to provoke him, the more he found her actions adorable. But he pretended to be exasperated for her benefit. He was an actor, after all, and skilled at pretending. Deep down, though, Axel was glad to be the one helping Maddie. He was glad she had called him and not someone else. Hours before, he had wondered what he could do for her.

After he got Maddie settled and called his mom to check on her, Axel had begun reading *A Summer's Dream*. He read all the way to the end until his eyes burned, begging for sleep. He was hooked. Hooked and already seeing himself in the lead role. He couldn't wait to talk to Maddie about the script once she was better.

But right now, Maddie had a different kind of need.

One he was too happy to fulfill.

Axel paused. He was tired, practically sleepwalking, but he enjoyed every mundane task that came with taking care of his assistant. He would cut out his tongue before admitting it to anyone, but Axel liked seeing her in his bed. Her body was engulfed by the thick blanket and the king-size mattress. He had other rooms, but Maddie deserved the best room in the house.

He hadn't felt anything like this with Natasha. That's how he knew he wasn't ready for marriage. So, what did his waiting on Maddie mean? his mind teased. Axel shoved that question aside. It didn't mean anything. Maddie was different. Like fam.

But she wasn't. Family, that is.

But she was a friend.

A good one to him. And a faithful assistant.

Helping her was a pleasure.

He whistled and strolled into the kitchen, intending to make pasta with creamy tomato sauce for lunch. He didn't cook much, but when he did, he found the process relaxing. Axel put on a pot of water to boil and then retrieved a large cooking pan and placed it on the stove. Then he searched through the cupboards and refrigerator for tomato sauce, heavy whipping cream, minced garlic, Italian seasoning, butter and brown sugar.

Gathering his salt and pepper grinder, Axel combined all the ingredients in the pan. After seasoning it to taste, Axel snapped his fingers, realizing he had forgotten to get the shredded Parmesan cheese. By this time, the water for the pasta was boiling with a fury. He added rigatoni to the water and then proceeded to add the Parmesan cheese to the sauce before turning off the burner. Once the pasta was ready, he drained it and added it to the creamy sauce, loving how the melted Parmesan folded around the pasta.

He sniffed. The aroma from the food filled the house, and his stomach growled. He was going to enjoy this. He dished up two bowls, one for himself and one for Maddie, and rested the food on the table. Then he went to get Maddie. She would want to hobble her way into the kitchen, but Axel intended to carry her.

Readying himself for more protests, Axel entered his room, only to find her asleep. She was lying on her side, her head resting on her hand, her mouth open. He stood over her and smiled when she snored. Her long lashes rested like a fan on her cheeks, and her hair was free, wild, crazy…and totally touchable. Without thinking, Axel reached over to play with her curls and caress her cheek before giving himself a mental slap and stepping back. Making physical contact while helping Maddie was one thing, but touching her just because was…unacceptable.

Tempting. But unacceptable.

And it created a frisson of fear in his heart.

His reaction had been involuntary, unplanned. That scared him. Many ad-libbed lines and actions in movies led to greatness. He couldn't do this in real life. He needed to respect the boundaries, stay on the other side of the line when it came to Maddie. He stole another glance, his eyes resting on her moist lips.

He swallowed, wondering if she tasted as sweet as she looked. There was only one way to find out. He gasped.

Speaking of taste… Axel snapped his fingers and ran back into the kitchen, where he had left his lunch. He covered Maddie's food, sat at the table alone and began to eat, scolding himself for the traitorous thoughts that had filled his head. Thoughts of kissing Maddie. Thoughts that must be due to the fact that he hadn't been with a woman in weeks. Six? Eight? He'd lost count.

Natasha had been away filming another movie, and he had been busy promoting *The Mantis*. In short, it had been a while. No wonder he was fantasizing about kissing Maddie. She was wrapped up under the covers in his bed. That was understandable.

It made sense.

He licked some of the sauce from the corner of his mouth.

Maybe he needed to scroll through his cell phone and see whom he could call. Then he dismissed that idea. Axel had deleted the contact information for his past hookups once he had entered a committed relationship with Natasha. And he wasn't about to venture into the DMs of his social media pages.

Actually, he *couldn't*.

Maddie had locked those down, closing his inboxes to comments. Here he was back to Maddie again. His mind had come full circle.

Axel laughed. If he told Maddie this, she would bop him on the head, wrinkle her nose and call him a conceited idiot. That's why they were friends. Only friends. And he respected her for that.

After finishing up his meal, Axel washed his hands and decided to check his schedule. Joni had texted him about the upcoming movie premiere. She wanted to know if he had heard from Natasha and if he had a date. His response was, "No and no." Joni had urged him to get a date, not to go alone. She didn't want him looking like he was pining after Natasha. That wouldn't do well for his sexy superhero image.

Axel sighed. Everything was about image.

He knew public perception was important, but it wasn't everything. It wasn't real. It was a mirage. Fact was, he didn't mind being alone. And with family. He raised his chin. He could take Maddie with him. She was safe. She was fun. He would ask her. She would enjoy the chance to dress up and hang with the stars.

Especially if he told her his friend and fellow thespian Michael B. Jordan would be there. That would sweeten the deal.

His mind made up, Axel broached the topic once she woke up and they sat around the kitchen table, after he had plied Maddie with some of the delicious, creamy pasta.

Licking her lips and rescuing some dangling cheese from her chin, Maddie asked, "Why do you want me to go when you have hundreds—no, thousands—of women ready to be a stand-in to replace Natasha?"

"Why not you?"

Maddie appeared to consider his words and then said, "Sure, I'll go."

Axel wrinkled his nose. "Why are you agreeing so easy?"

"Artie Rae will be there."

He shook his head, still not having a clue.

"He's the one who needs the intern," she said. "It would be a great time to meet my new boss and see Michael B. Jordan." She wiggled her hips. "It might be my lucky night in more than one way."

"He's taken. Michael B. Jordan, that is," Axel felt compelled to say. He had a sudden urge to take back his offer for her to accompany him.

"Dating isn't taken," she said, pointing at him. "Look at you and Natasha."

"Ouch. That's cold."

She looked contrite. "Sorry. That's not what I meant. I meant that a week or two ago, you were both America's darlings, and look at you now." She popped some of the pasta in her mouth. "Well, she still is, but you aren't.

"Oh goodness," she said, slapping a hand over her mouth. "I'm coming off real insensitive. I'm sorry. I'd better keep my mouth shut and keep eating." With that, she put another spoonful of the pasta in her mouth.

"It's all good," Axel said, trying not to be distracted by the grease on her lips—and not to think again about kissing her. "I'm not hurt by the breakup. The public scorn hurts more than the end of our relationship."

"Wow." Her brows raised. "Now that's cold."

She was right. "You know what? Let's move on to another topic, because nothing I'm saying is coming out the way I mean." He knew why, too. He was struggling with a surge of jealousy rising within him. Jealousy at the thought of Maddie trying to cozy up to the other actor and her new boss.

"Tell me about this internship," he said, going to the refrigerator to get a bottle of water.

She gave him a look filled with suspicion. "Why? I don't want you messing this up for me. Not that you could, because I have a solid in with Artie."

"I'm interested in anything you want to do," he quipped in a light tone, though he was very serious. And curious about her "in with Artie." She sounded pretty sure, like she had nailed the internship, even though, to his knowledge, she hadn't even interviewed yet.

"Oh." She rested her fork in the bowl and wiped her mouth. "It's a science fiction romance that plays with time and long-lost loves."

"That sounds intriguing," he said, handing her a bottle of water.

"I think so, too. At first, I was hesitant, but now I'm looking forward to it. It's great experience, and one step toward my becoming a director. I'll be thirty soon, and it's time I establish myself."

Her words resonated within him, and Axel chided himself for his selfishness. He could hear from her dreamy tone that Maddie was ready to embrace a new beginning. He couldn't be the oaf blocking her path. Now he was jealous for a different reason—he should have been the one to help her get through the door and beside the director's seat. Not this nameless hookup. Axel returned to his seat across from her and took her hand. "By the time I was thirty, I had already banked millions. I get it. You're right to go for it. How can I help?"

She cocked her head. "You mean that?"

Axel nodded.

"Why the sudden change of heart?"

"I care about you, and I want the best for you," Axel said. He drummed his fingers on the table. "Now, do you need me to give Artie a call and insist he hires you?"

She chuckled. "Nope. That's totally not necessary. I wouldn't mind a written reference, though."

"Cool. Go ahead and write it and I'll sign."

This time Maddie cracked up.

"What's so funny?" he asked.

"Nothing. I'll do that," she said, her eyes bright. "I suppose you want me to pick out my birthday gift as well? Like I usually do."

"Why not? It's one less thing I have to think about and one less thing I get wrong," he shot back, causing Maddie to laugh even harder.

"Axel Harrington. There is only one you. No one like you, and I am going to miss you."

"I'm going to miss you, too," he said. "Just promise me one thing. You'll interview your replacement? I don't think I'll find another you, but it's worth a try."

Chapter Thirteen

She should be pleased. Pleased that Axel wasn't fighting her resignation. Pleased he was supporting her pursuing the next step in her career.

Instead, Maddie stood in her condo, gazing through the window, battling dual feelings of jealousy and misery while she waited for Axel to arrive. It had been raining all day, and the weather coincided with her mood. Axel had executed a U-turn and was now pushing her to find him a new assistant. Nagging her about whether she had reviewed the applicants' résumés. That was the topic of conversation when they weren't working with the students.

The only thing that kept her from blasting him to quit yammering on about her departure was the fact that along with the nagging, Axel had taken great care of her foot. He had made her soak in Epsom salts and had massaged her with a blend of healing oils before giving her toes a fresh coat. She was sure his careful ministrations were the reasons she was now out of the brace a few days later and in a pair of flip-flops that looked like zombie feet.

Her new venture awaited, and she had plenty to do besides looking at the passersby in the parking lot outside her building. She had already spoken to Artie and had secured the internship. They would meet up at Axel's movie premiere to finalize the plans. She should be ecstatic. She should be packing. Keri had purchased her a set of Michael Kors luggage and her mother had sent another box with clothes and shoes.

And, yes, she should be conducting interviews.

Yet Maddie found herself stalling. Stalling and try-ing to get past this inexplicable hurt she felt. It was for that reason that Axel was on his way to her place to decide on four applicants to interview. He had tossed out that he just wanted to get it done. Maddie had agreed, but it was like Axel was eager to replace her.

As if she was replaceable. And she didn't like it.

She released a huge sigh. She had six days left, and then she would be done with Axel. Forever. Okay, *forever* sounded a bit dramatic, but Maddie doubted they would be in the same circles or remain in touch. The two years she'd worked for him would be forgot-ten, wiped away like sauce on a table. He was the big leagues, on the A-list, and she was the runt of the lit-ter. No—the straggling duckling.

He pulled into the lot, and Maddie blinked to keep the stupid tears at bay.

When she opened her front door, he was all smiles and holding a cheesecake Tanya had made and sent with love—a sign that his mother was feeling better. She was irritated at his movie star–handsome face, since she had spent a good portion of her early morning attacking a large pimple on her cheek. One that appeared after she had devoured a pint of mint chocolate chip ice cream. Its presence had been further amplified by one of the teens in the drama class—the young man had even dubbed it Pimpy.

Really? Nicknaming her pimple? Her mouth quirked into a grin. She had to admit that was funny. But she wanted Pimpy gone.

Axel sauntered into her home with the swagger of someone who owned the place and rested the cheesecake on the counter.

"How's your foot?" he asked.

"It's fine," she said before resting her hands on the granite countertop. "Are you ready to begin?"

He nodded. "If you are."

Heading to her couch, they divided the stack of résumés Joni had emailed and then each decided on three. From those six, they argued until they narrowed it down to four. Three women and one man. Maddie found herself rooting for Lindsay or Tim—with a heavy lean toward Tim. Like Lindsay, he had an undergraduate degree and some experience as a celebrity assistant. Tim wanted to help his ailing parents, and that tugged at Maddie's heart. She had spoken to her mother much more often over the past few days and treasured that time with Faran. Lindsay, on the other hand, was driven, ambitious and gorgeous. She looked like she belonged on a runway, having dyed her hair a bold red.

But it all came down to the interview. Maddie intended to be impartial and make the right decision on the best person for Axel. The one who wouldn't be in awe of him and who would keep him organized and manage his appointments.

Axel slapped his hands on his jeans. "By this time tomorrow, I'll have a new assistant. Hopefully she'll be able to start right away so you can get her trained."

Maddie raised her brow.

"Or he," Axel amended, flexing his muscles under his shirt.

"If you need me to hang on a little longer..." Maddie trailed off.

Axel shook his head. "No. No. I won't take advantage of you by asking you to stay." He said it in a tone that was meant to reassure her. But all it did was make her secret misery multiply. On the outside, she placed a wide grin on her face.

"Okay, that's good to know," she said, holding her smile in place.

Axel stood and stretched. "Did you decide on your dress, jewelry and stylist as yet? The premiere is mere days away, and it's tough getting the best in the business at the last minute."

"Yes, don't worry about a thing," she said, also

getting to her feet. "I've got it covered." Maddie had invited the best person she knew to help her get ready.

He made a point to look at her footwear. "I'm hoping you'll be a little more...conventional."

She snickered. "Conventional is for old folks. I promise you, when you see me, you'll be dazzled." Maddie hid a smile when she saw the doubt on his face. The day of his premiere, her last official day of work, was one they both would remember. That was a guarantee.

"All right, big talker. I hope you put my money where your mouth is," he joked.

"I sure did. And then some."

Axel left to go visit with his mother. It was the weekend, and he was going Jet Skiing with Caleb and Hawk in Miami Beach, where Hawk lived. He appeared to be excited about their adventure. Maddie was happy for him. This time out of the spotlight was great for his psyche.

She heard the lock click and waited in the hallway for Keri to walk inside.

Her roommate trotted in, full of energy. "Hey, girlfriend. Are you staying off that foot?" To look at her, one would never know that Keri had flown to Philadelphia and back that day. Eyeing the coffee cup in her hand, Maddie figured Keri had stocked up on enough coffee to keep her wired for the night.

"Yes, I am." Maddie headed toward the couch again, knowing Keri would join her.

"Where's your shadow?" she asked.

Maddie's mouth dropped. "You wrong for that.

Axel isn't my shadow. It's the other way around. I get paid for it, too, so it's not all bad."

"Keep telling yourself that," Keri said, wagging a finger at her. "That man is so into you, he won't know what to do with himself when you're off to better and grander things."

"Please. You couldn't be further from the truth. He's more excited than I am about my gig with Artie. He's practically pushing me out the door." She meant to sound humorous, but the sadness she felt crept into her tone.

Keri's face melted with compassion. "Are you going to be okay? You look like you're going through withdrawals."

"I think I am," Maddie confessed. "I'm going to miss him. While he can't wait to be rid of me."

"Oh, honey. I don't think that's the case. You said yourself he didn't want to hold you back."

"I know," Maddie said. "But it would be nice if he felt the loss like I am."

"He's an actor. I think he's putting on a big show for your benefit."

"You think so?" Maddie hated how hopeful she sounded.

"Yeah…" Keri fiddled with her uniform. "Why is his attitude bugging you? I asked you this before, and I have to ask again." She cocked her head. "Do you have feelings for Axel?"

"He's a movie star. Almost every woman is in love with him." Maddie hedged. She massaged her neck, suddenly feeling constricted.

"I mean Axel the man. The one behind the glamour. The one you get to know on an intimate level, in a way that no one else does."

She touched her chest. "I care about him, but I don't think my feelings go beyond that." Yeah, right. She had snuggled in his bed, inhaled his scent and for an odd moment wondered what it would be like if he had joined her.

"I think you do know, but you don't want to admit it. You don't want to bring your feelings to the surface because then you'd have to face your insecurities."

Maddie gasped. Keri's blunt words had hit their mark.

Keri shot to her feet. "But what do I know? I'm exhausted and an undercover romantic. I enjoy rooting for the underdog."

Underdog? Maddie scrunched her nose. She didn't know if she appreciated being viewed that way. She was strong and capable. But Keri was only pointing out how Maddie herself felt.

"I don't see you as an underdog," Keri rushed to clarify. She bent over and chucked Maddie under her chin. "But I know you see yourself that way when it comes to Axel, though it's the furthest thing from the truth. You have a glow, a style that's all your own, and you walk around with your head high. You refuse to be placed in a mold, to let society define you. That's intimidating to other women. And possibly to most men. But Axel isn't like most men. He's drawn to you. You don't see the way he looks at you."

"Whatever. You're being a loyal friend," Maddie said, brushing off Keri's words and pushing her glasses up on her face.

"Just wait until he sees you in that dress you picked out. You're going to have to scoop his tongue up off the floor."

Maddie laughed, but on the inside she feared that very thing happening. She didn't want Axel to be wowed by what was on the outside. She wanted him to be wowed with her now. As she was in her natural state. As she was with him.

Because she was super wowed by Axel Harrington. Somewhere over the past week, with his tenderness toward her, a crush had blossomed. A crush she found normal; she could live with it. But the rate of its development, its fast spread toward her heart—that worried her.

That made her know that leaving was the best thing to do.

Chapter Fourteen

"Are you going to tell her that you don't want her to leave?" Tanya asked, using her shears to trim her rosebushes. It was close to 6:00 p.m., and it wasn't raining on this side of town. Tanya was taking advantage of that by tending to her prized roses. She had on a pair of jeans, a long-sleeved shirt and a straw hat.

Axel had arrived at her home to check on her, but his mother was inquiring about him, his welfare.

"I can't do that, Mom. It would be selfish, and I'd be holding her back." He didn't bother hiding the truth from his mother. She knew him. Saw past his act. Saw his misery. He moved to help her by tending to one of the other trees. He loved spending this time out here with his mom. None of his brothers were around, and his father was still at the district office.

"Your feelings matter. And maybe they would make a difference," Tanya said, bending over to pluck at a weed.

He shook his head and wiped the sweat off his brow. "I can't lay a guilt trip to make her stay." Even though he answered to the contrary, he wondered about his mother's use of the word *feelings*. The feelings he talked about were those of a friend, nothing more. But she was making it sound like it was more than that.

Tanya nodded and rubbed her chin. "Actually, you're right. She should go. But you need to join her."

Axel reared back. His mother's statement had caught him off guard. "What do you mean?"

"You told me about her script and how you loved it. What about being an executive producer and funding her project?"

He paused. That idea had merit. He had read her script again and had been bowled over by the intensity of the characters. Maddie had penned a raw, gritty tale, giving the lead a depth and room to grow. A lead she'd envisioned he would play.

Axel couldn't believe she viewed him in that light. But his heart constricted, knowing the level of her faith in his ability to draw deep within himself and bring the script to life.

"That's a great idea." It was one he had thought of himself.

"Put your money where your heart is," Tanya said.

Whoa. His heart? His mother was going a bit too far with that thinking. "I don't know if I would say all that, but it would be a good investment," Axel said. "She's amazing with the students. You should see her in action. Maddie's got a way about her. I'm the celebrity, but she's the one they gravitate toward. The school play is going to be a huge success."

"You realize your face lights up when you talk about her?"

"Well, that's because she's a great person," Axel said, hiding his face from her view. His mother was studying him with a level of scrutiny that alarmed him. "I can acknowledge Maddie's awesomeness without it meaning that I have deeper feelings for her. It's possible for men and women to be platonic friends. We can maintain a professional relationship based on mutual respect and admiration."

"Yeah, but not in your case. You're content to bask in that river called denial."

"Why is everyone insisting there is more to this than what I'm saying?" Axel grunted with frustration. "Drake and Hawk were teasing me about this the other day, and I don't like it."

"Your brothers and I see how you are with her as clear as we see the freckles on your face. You're hooked, and the quicker you accept it, the faster you can hold on to her before someone else does." She dusted her hands on her jeans.

That was his exit cue. Tanya seemed fixated on his nonexistent love affair. Kissing the top of her head, Axel made his mother promise not to overdo it after she declined his offer to pay for a gardener.

On his drive home, his mother's words taunted

him. Tanya truly thought he was in love. Yes, he could admit that he found Maddie desirable, but that was the extent of his interest. It was entirely physical. He found himself fascinated with her lips and ached to get a taste. Imagining that was his new pastime. But beyond that, once Maddie was out of his life, all that would fade. He would get a new assistant and life would go on.

If she crossed his mind, he would send her a text to check on her, maybe give a friendly five-minute call. And that was a big if.

Putting on the radio to drown out his mother's words from his mind, Axel sang at the top of his lungs until he received a call from his agent.

"What's up, Ralph?" he asked, sitting at a light.

"Guess what, buddy? Have I got some good news for you," Ralph said, his voice booming throughout the vehicle. Axel turned down the volume. "Netflix called. They have a script—a drama—and they want you to play it. You're their second choice. Their first bailed during negotiations."

Axel leaned forward. "A drama?" He didn't care that he wasn't first choice. He was just glad to have been considered.

"Yes. It's a cross between heartwarming and tearjerker. It's about a retired football player who learns he has a child. A child who lost her mom and who needs him. He struggles with depression and drinking but has to overcome all that to keep her out of the foster care system. It's tentatively titled *The Father She Needs*."

"Wow. Tell me more," Axel said, intrigued. His heart raced in his chest, and he slapped the wheel. Finally. Something with substance. "I can't believe they want me." The light changed, and he pressed on the gas, careful not to speed.

"They do, and they're quite willing to pay you a boatload if you agree. They're eager to get started, so that's something to think about."

If he agreed? *If* he agreed? This was a no-brainer. But experience had taught him caution. A good concept didn't always translate into a good screenplay. "Send me the script," he said. "I'll read through it tonight and get back to you."

"Will do. Look out for it."

As soon as he got off the phone, Axel called Maddie. Her response was just as enthusiastic. "I'm stoked for you. This is your chance to show you're more than your magnificent body."

She thought his body was magnificent? Axel straightened and puffed his chest.

"Ralph is sending over the script for me to read. Netflix wants to begin filming soon, so I have to make up my mind. The plot sounds like something I can sink my teeth into, and if the screenplay delivers, then I am jumping in with both feet."

"There you go." Her voice held a hint of longing.

Realization dawned. Axel could have smacked himself for his thoughtlessness. "By the way, I read your script," he said. "Read it twice, actually."

"You did?" She sounded hopeful and then drew in a deep breath. "What did you think?"

"I'm thinking…" He trailed off on purpose.

"What? Spit it out," she said.

He entered the roundabout and turned on a street that would take him back to Maddie's place. "I'm heading over there. I'll tell you then."

"Wait. I can't wait—"

He ended the call with a chuckle. Maddie was so impatient. If he knew her, she was going to be in the parking lot when he arrived, tapping her feet. Sure enough, she was exactly where he'd predicted, with her arms folded. As soon as she saw him, she dashed toward his car.

Chapter Fifteen

"I can't believe you left me hanging like that," Maddie said once Axel had arrived.

He came out the car, laughing and pointing at her. "I knew you would be here. Do I know my Maddie or what?"

Wait. *His* Maddie?

Her eyes narrowed. But Axel hadn't seemed to notice his choice of words. His eyes flashed. "I loved your script. You wrote a character any serious actor would want to portray. Your screenplay has Academy Award written all over it."

Maddie's mouth dropped. "That's some high praise."

"It's the truth."

She licked her lips, afraid to ask the next question but knowing she must. Gathering her courage, she asked. "Does this mean you might want to…um…" She cleared her throat and wiped her brow. "Can you picture yourself playing Brock?"

Axel nodded. "I would be honored."

Maddie screamed. She couldn't believe it. She raced over to Axel and snatched him close to her. "I can't believe it. This is wonderful." She kissed his cheek, appreciating the feel of his bulging muscles. He was rock solid. "Axel, I can't believe you read *A Summer's Dream* and liked it," she purred.

He patted her back. "I really did."

She basked in his arms for a moment before a tingling sensation traveled through her body. Her senses were coming alive at being in Axel's arms, alarming her.

Just then, a thought occurred. One that put an arrow in her enthusiasm.

Stepping out of his arms, she peered up at him. "Are you just saying this because you don't want me to leave?"

His eyes widened. "Why would I do that?" His smile faded, and he backed away. "Is that how you see me? You think I'd manipulate you in that way? Can't you see that I'm changing?"

Shame filled her. "I'm sorry," she said, wringing her fingers. "The thought came and I—"

"You ran with it. Instead of stopping to think." Axel shook his head. He opened the door to his truck. "I'm going to leave before I say something I regret."

"Axel, don't leave. I put my foot in my mouth."

"Naw. I'm good. I can't be around you right now."

He stuck one leg into the truck. "Do you need a ride tomorrow or can you drive?"

Maddie gave a jerky nod, sorry she had spoiled their celebration with her doubt. Why had she done that? It was like she'd wanted to sabotage their moment. "I'm sorry," she whispered.

"You don't have to keep apologizing," he said, his tone aloof and impersonal. "If you can, bring me a couple cups of coffee when you come to the school tomorrow morning. I'll be up most of the night reading *The Father She Needs*, and I'm going to need the caffeine."

"I can do that," she said quietly.

Seconds later, Axel was gone. She stood in that spot, rooted by her regret, for a good twenty minutes. If she hadn't felt raindrops, Maddie might have stayed out there even longer. The weather was as mercurial as her mood. She trudged into her house and stopped at the mirror in her entryway.

Facing herself, she said, "This is more than attraction. You like him."

No, her mind raged, trying to twist the truth like a ball of twine. But Maddie wasn't having it. "You do like him. Admit it." Her face crumpled, and she could only nod, cupping her mouth with her hand. This wasn't a crush. Or attraction. This was something more. Something that could build into love if she allowed it. Panic engulfed her. Her chest heaved. Maddie closed her eyes.

Six days. Six days. Then she could run. She would run and not look back.

And in time, these ridiculous fantasies, this sense-less emotion she refused to label would fade. Then she could breathe. Opening her eyes, Maddie looked at her reflection. When she saw Axel tomorrow, she would have to be very careful. She couldn't let any-thing she was thinking or feeling show in her man-nerisms or in her expression. Axel could be very observant, and she didn't want him noticing that she was enamored with him. All she had to do was act normal.

Act normal. Act normal. Act normal...

That was her mantra all through the night and the next morning. She entered the auditorium with a bright smile and handed him his coffees. Axel ac-cepted them and thanked her before directing his at-tention to the script.

He discussed the scenes they would cover that day with her before the bell rang and the students filed inside. Maddie gave them her attention, giving them pointers. She kept up the cheerful demeanor, wear-ing it like an armor to cover her misery. It made her exhausted. Acting was definitely not her forte.

Axel, on the other hand, thrived. The students gave him their rapt attention, and even Maddie got caught up whenever he assumed a role to show the students what to do. Thankfully, he hadn't asked her to reprise her role as Maria to his Captain Von Trapp. Maddie wouldn't have been able to keep up the pretense. That would have been too much for her emotional well-being. A strain on her control. Especially since Axel had been cool and his stance unaffected all day.

When they parted ways at the end of the day, Maddie entered her car and flopped against the steering wheel. She wanted to go home and hide under the covers, but she couldn't. She had to head over to Axel's house and interview her three prospective replacements. One had already called to say she had accepted another position. At the time, holding the interviews at his larger place had seemed like a good idea. Not so much now that they were at odds.

After ordering takeout that she waited for about thirty minutes in curbside parking to get, she drove over to Axel's house. She used her spare key to enter, and the smell of fresh-baked cookies assailed her nostrils. She inhaled, her mouth watering at the idea of the treat. Oh, Axel wasn't playing fair. He knew how much she adored gooey chocolate chip cookies. She followed her nose to the kitchen.

Sure enough, Axel stood behind the cookies he must have just taken out the oven and transferred to the cooling rack. He held a supersize one in his hand. She could see he had already bitten a chunk out of it, chocolate staining the side of his mouth. Maddie placed the takeout on the counter and looked at him. The smirk on his face was a sign he knew exactly what he was doing. Well, if he thought she was going to ask him for a cookie, then he was thinking right.

Maddie had no shame. She knew Axel had this cookie dough special ordered from somewhere—maybe Belgium.

Placing a hand on her hip, she asked, "So this is how you do me?"

"You're welcome to some," he said, his tone formal. He could have been talking to a stranger.

Maddie stomped her foot. "Would you quit being so polite? It's grating on my nerves."

"I will stop if you stop judging me," he shot back, his eyes flashing with fury.

"I said I was sorry already. What more can I do?" she yelled, holding out her arm. "Do you want some of my blood? What's your blood type?"

Axel stood frozen for a second before he busted out laughing. "You're so dramatic. I had no idea you had it in you."

She rolled her eyes. "Whatever." She shoved the takeout his way. "I bought you dinner, but it appears you're bent on spoiling your appetite. You baked those cookies to get back at me. Admit it."

"Yes, I did," he said, coming around to poke her on the nose. "Seeing you lose it was well worth it. I don't think I've ever seen you in such a tizzy."

"It's a crying shame that the world's sexiest man would use one of the most corny words in the English language such as *tizzy*."

He placed a finger over her mouth. "Keep it between us."

Maddie's breath caught. His finger smelled like delectable chocolate. She stuck her tongue out and grazed his finger before popping her tongue back in her mouth. Her eyes went wide. Now why had she done that?

Axel snatched his finger away and drew close into

her personal space, his chest heaving and his eyes dark with...desire?

They stood together, defenses down, studying each other, wary, wondering what their next move should be. Maddie was afraid to release a breath, to ruin the moment. She reached up to wrap her hair around her finger just to keep her hands from reaching out to explore Axel's chest.

He lifted his hand, a finger grazing her cheek. "Maddie, what are you doing to me?" He bent his head, his eyes on her lips. Maddie's stomach muscles clenched from the knowledge that Axel was about to kiss her. Her eyes fluttered closed.

Axel jumped back.

The doorbell rang. It took a moment for her mind to register the intrusion. The rescue? Because she had been about to do something stupid, like act on her fantasy, her growing attraction.

"The first interviewee is here," he said, sounding normal. She, on the other hand, was still trying to capture her breath and slow her racing pulse.

Maddie walked toward the door, then opened it to greet Tim, barely covering her annoyance that he was five minutes early. Gathering her composure, Maddie introduced herself and Axel before leading the man into Axel's office. Axel sauntered in, holding a plate of food. Tim appeared awestruck.

Tim wasn't able to answer her questions because he was too busy glancing over at Axel, who was chomping away in another corner of the room. Maddie pressed through, but Tim interrupted the interview to ask Axel for a selfie and an autograph. Maddie showed Tim to the door, not even trying to hide her disappointment.

"Well, that was gruesome," Axel said.

"You did that on purpose," Maddie accused, pushing her glasses up on her nose.

Axel blinked. "From the moment he entered the house, I could tell he wasn't the one."

She pursed her lips. "Yeah, right."

"I knew within fifteen seconds of meeting you I was going to hire you," Axel said, pinning her with his gaze. "I knew you were special, and I was right."

The tension between them escalated. Maddie cleared her throat. "Axel, about what happened before... I, ah, I shouldn't have done that."

"What?" he shrugged. "Licked my finger? It's nothing. Light banter between friends."

Her eyes narrowed. So, he was just going to pretend like he hadn't been about to press his lips on hers. Maddie knew she hadn't imagined that. Axel arched a brow, challenging her to disagree. Maybe he was ashamed to admit his attraction. That stung.

She swung around and went to get her takeout. Maddie managed to eat half of it before the doorbell rang again. This time, Axel opened the door, and a young woman entered. Maddie struggled to recall her name. She had to peek at the résumé. Marsha.

Marsha had a mouselike voice. She was both deferential and timid. Maddie ended the interview after five minutes. Marsha wouldn't last a day with a man of Axel's temperament. One yell and Marsha would disintegrate like a marshmallow in hot cocoa.

That left Lindsay.

When Lindsay arrived, she shook Maddie's hand with confidence, whipping her hair like she knew she had the job. She was tall, athletic and even more stunning in person. She had fire and spunk, and she didn't seem impressed by Axel's presence.

Most important, Axel liked her. Maddie could tell. He even took over the interview, the two bonding over football. Within minutes, he and Lindsay were laughing like they had known each other for years.

Maddie shrank into her chair and watched Lindsay work her charm. Lindsay knew all Axel's films and had strong critiques for him. From under her lashes, Maddie could see that Axel was lapping up every word. Lindsay had captured his mind. And his complete attention. Half an hour later, Axel was sharing his cookies with Lindsay. *Her* cookies.

Maddie hadn't even had one yet. Before Lindsay departed, Axel offered Lindsay the position without consulting her.

He walked Lindsay out to her car and came back, his mouth in a wide smile. "She can start tomorrow. Isn't that great?"

"What's great about it?" Maddie folded her arms and glared. "I thought you wanted me to do the interviews."

"What does it matter?" he answered with a shrug. "I'm the one who's going to work with her. And I like her. It's like talking with one of my brothers. She'll suit me well."

"Hmm," Maddie said, twisting her lips, jealousy churning with the rage of a washing machine. "So, this has nothing to do with the fact that she's gorgeous?"

Another shrug. "I didn't notice."

As if. Whatever.

Maddie grabbed the remaining cookies and stuffed them in a Ziploc bag before storming out of Axel's home. She ate three on her way home and the rest once she was in bed. The sugar overload made her have to drink water, which led to multiple trips to the bathroom. And a tummy ache. As a result, Maddie entered the school the next morning with bags under her eyes.

Lindsay was already there, sucking up to Axel. She looked refreshed and eager. And energetic. The students surrounded her, entranced by her charisma.

Maddie sighed, dropping into one of the chairs. She yawned and wondered if she should go home. She couldn't fault the kids. Lindsay was perfect. Perfect in ways she wasn't. Maddie had been replaced with perfection. Axel wouldn't have a problem saying goodbye now.

But you know what? Maddie being upstaged was a thing of the past. Being Faran's daughter had prepared her for women like Lindsay.

She had five more days. Five days to do her thang. And that's what she would do. She was still very much Axel's assistant, and she would do a bang-up job until the very end. And she would make sure Lindsay was ready to take over for Axel once she was gone.

Now that she had her mind right and her confidence in check, Maddie went to work.

Chapter Sixteen

"Did you get a chance to review the contract?"
Ralph asked. He had flown to Florida from Los Angeles to meet up with Axel and had arrived at Axel's house a little after 4:00 p.m. Axel had suggested they wait until he was in Los Angeles for the premiere, but Ralph must have sensed his hesitation and knew Axel would need some convincing.

They sat by the dining room table, and Axel tried to remain attentive as Ralph explained all the components of the document. Netflix had agreed to Axel's demands of not baring his chest or revealing any other body parts. There was a shower scene that did nothing to move the story forward, and they had agreed to eliminate it. He only had one qualm.

"Everything looks good. I only have one minor

problem. I see that filming starts in a week, close to Maddie's birthday and the performance night for the drama club. Can they push the start date?" Though she wouldn't be his employee anymore, Maddie had promised to stay in town until after the play. She would use six days to pack and to get ready for her move to Oregon.

Ralph shook his head. "They are taking a chance on you. Putting off production isn't a good look. You're going to have to decide what's more important—your career or pleasing some kids."

Axel rested his hand on his head. He didn't like that he had to make a choice. "Just call and ask. Let them know I had a prior commitment."

Taking off his wire-rimmed glasses and rubbing his eyes, Ralph squared off with Axel. "I can't believe we're even having this conversation. You said you want to be respected as an actor and you have the role of a lifetime in your lap, yet you're asking me to see if you can stall. Get a later start date."

"I promised those children I'd be there. Both they and Maddie would never forgive me."

Gathering the script, Ralph stood. "I'll call. I'm sure they'll agree to appease the demands of an A-list actor, though they are already behind due to cast changes." He tapped the table. "Just sign the contract."

"It's not a demand. It's a request." Axel stood and expelled a long breath. "I need a moment to process."

"Don't take too long," Ralph said, pointing to his Rolex. "As the saying goes, time is money." Everything about Ralph's tone suggested that he thought Axel should jump at this chance.

Axel pulled open the sliding doors and walked outside. There were dark storm clouds. Axel sniffed. He could smell the rain. It was coming, and it was going to be a serious downpour.

Stepping out a little farther, Axel walked out to the deck of his rental home and held on to the railing. He wished he could ask Maddie what she thought. But even Maddie had chosen her career over him. Okay, being his assistant was the bottom rung. She did need to make a vertical move. He couldn't compare that with his decision.

If Netflix didn't agree and he lost this role, there would be others… Maybe.

No, Axel had to be honest with himself. He wanted this part, and Ralph was right. Scripts like this were hard to find. He needed to think long-term. He needed to take this gig. Maybe he should keep the original production date. Not make a fuss.

The drama students would understand, he told himself. Especially if he secured them special premiere tickets to his movie. Yeah, that's what he would do. He would keep the original date and make it up to them. Once he had made up his mind, Axel strode into the house and signed the contract. He did push for Ralph to ask for another start date.

Ralph agreed, gripped the contract and thumped Axel on the back. "That's the Axel I know. You're right to think of yourself. You had me worried there for a hot minute. Let me scan these and email them to the producers."

"Hang on a minute," Axel said. He strode into his room and retrieved Maddie's script. "When you hand in the contract, can you submit this script for consideration?"

Ralph raised a brow. "That's not how it's done."

"I know. But all you can get is a yes or no."

"I like the way you think," Ralph said, stuffing the script in his suitcase. Then he rushed through the door as if he was afraid Axel would change his mind regarding the contract.

Standing by the front door, watching Ralph pull out of his driveway, Axel shoved his hands in his pockets. His stomach churned. He wasn't looking forward to breaking the news to the students the next day. They were going to be disappointed. And Maddie. He dreaded seeing Maddie's face most of all.

A couple of hours later, Axel sat on the couch in his living room watching a football game on television. Well, he was trying to watch, but his mind couldn't focus. He was consumed by his decision to sign the contract and bail on the kids.

Hearing thunder crack, Axel looked outside and saw that it was pitch-dark. He decided to turn the station to the weather channel. Love Creek was under a hurricane watch. Hurricane Shelley had hit land and was making her way up the coast. Schools had already been canceled the next day as a precaution. Having grown up in Florida, Axel wasn't too alarmed. He knew there was a strong possibility for clear skies and sunshine the next day. The weather was just that temperamental. He prayed he would still be able to travel out that weekend.

Axel sent quick texts to his siblings and parents. Each had houses that were built to withstand Category 5 winds. They texted back that they were all fine and had enough supplies to last until the end of the year.

Relieved, Axel texted Maddie next to check on her. She replied,

I'm good. I'm not in a flood zone so I'm not worried.

Her words put his mind at ease, so Axel returned to watching the game. He was about to drift off to sleep, but at about 10:00 p.m., his doorbell rang. Axel peered through the peephole. It was pouring outside.

It was Lindsay. She stood shivering on his doorstep. He scrunched his nose. He hadn't recalled asking her to come by, but maybe her showing up was a sign. He would see what she thought about his missing the play.

"What brings you here?" he asked once he had let her inside, taking in her wet, stringy hair and soaked sandals. She wiped her feet on his doormat. But before she could answer, Axel waved a hand. "Before you answer that, let me ask your opinion on something." He scuttled into the kitchen with Lindsay shuffling behind him. She asked to use the restroom to freshen up, and Axel directed her to the half bath near the front of the house and told her to help herself to one of the towels on the rack.

She excused herself, and Axel used that opportunity to pull up his email on his laptop. Sure enough, Ralph had already emailed him a signed copy of the contract and confirmed that he had emailed it to Netflix, tagging Maddie and Joni on the email.

Lindsay returned and slipped onto the bar stool. She had pinned her hair into a ponytail. "So, what did you want to talk about? I'm all ears."

Axel quickly relayed his dilemma with the production start date being close to the night of the school play. Lindsay listened without interrupting until he was done. Axel liked that, though he couldn't tell what she was thinking by her facial expression. Maddie would have cut him off to ask some clarifying questions. Axel reprimanded himself not to compare the two women. There was no comparison. Maddie was Maddie. And Lindsay…well, he would get to know her.

Once he was done, Lindsay held out her hands. "You did the right thing. I completely cosign your decision."

"Really?" he asked, surprised by how decisive she sounded.

"Yeah. I'm glad to see you challenge yourself. Why settle?"

"Exactly," he said, pumping his fists. She got him. This was wonderful. Maddie would have chewed him out and clucked at him for choosing money over the children.

"Good. I was glad I could help," Lindsay said.

Axel smiled and nodded. But he had a niggling frisson of unease at how Lindsay had seemed to agree with him. Was that her opinion, or was she saying what she thought he wanted to hear? Axel didn't know her well enough to know. On second thought, he wouldn't have minded if she had argued with him a little, or at least asked him some questions about how he felt about his decision.

The way Maddie would have done...

Stop it, he told himself. He was being contrary. In a matter of days, Maddie would be leaving, and Lindsay was here... *Wait.* Why was she here in the middle of what could become a Category 2 hurricane? He had been focused on himself and hadn't questioned her unexpected appearance. Axel tilted his head and asked her the question.

"I wanted to drop off my references," she said, appearing pensive.

In the middle of torrential rains? His eyes narrowed. That was something she could have given him tomorrow. He went on high alert. No, Lindsay had another reason for coming.

When he didn't answer, she pulled her reference letters out of her purse and placed them on the counter. The air in the room grew tense, and Axel became wary. He hoped she wasn't a groupie in disguise. His mind registered that he was alone in his house with her, and if anything went down, it would be his word against hers. Lindsay stood and walked over to where he stood. That's when he realized her lashes were spiky from tears.

"What's wrong?" he asked, his concern outweighing his caution.

"I—" Her chin quivered, and she twisted her hands. "I don't have anywhere to live." The tears she had tried to hold back poured down her face.

Axel's compassion rose. "I don't understand. What's going on?"

"When I got called for this interview, I was down to my last hundred dollars, so I packed up everything and drove up here. I checked into the Days Inn. My parents didn't want me to leave, so they cut off my credit cards. When I got back to the hotel today, the hotel told me I had to vacate the room."

"Wow. That's harsh." Axel wasn't a parent, but he couldn't understand why someone would do that to their child, especially in the middle of bad weather. "I can't believe the manager turned you out in this hurricane."

"The lobby was packed with people who had driven here to ride out the hurricane. He told me he had to free up the room."

All Axel could do was shake his head. The lack of humanity appalled him.

Lindsay suddenly lunged against his chest and wrapped her arms about him, wetting his shirt with her tears. Her chest heaved from her sobs, but Axel stood still. He wouldn't reciprocate by touching her or returning the embrace, but he didn't want to be insensitive. Axel shifted and stepped back but kept his arms to his sides. Lindsay lifted her head and dragged her hands across her cheeks. Her face was red, and he could see the mortification on her face.

"I'm so sorry to barge in on you like this," she said, now unable to look him in the eyes. "I didn't know where else to go once the manager said I had to leave." She hiccuped. "I was going to stay in my car at a park, but when I saw the lightning and thunder, I knew I had to seek shelter."

He wanted to ask why she hadn't called Maddie or gone to a nearby school, but he didn't want to add to her obvious distress. Maybe she wasn't thinking straight. And she wasn't from the town to know where to go.

"No, I'm glad you came here instead of camping out in your vehicle," he said, though he wasn't. "You're now my employee, and I care about what happens to you."

Axel put some distance between them and offered her something to drink. Lindsay accepted and guzzled down a glass of juice like she hadn't eaten in days. He asked if she was hungry, and when she nodded, he fed her leftovers. While she ate, Axel called a few hotels, but they were all booked up. He checked a hotel booking site, but everything within twenty miles was sold out for that night. He did reserve her a room for a few days, but she could only check in the next day. So that left tonight.

Axel mulled over his options, observing the young woman from under his lashes. He couldn't turn her out.

After a few minutes, Axel made up his mind. He

knew what he had to do. He cleared his throat and offered, "You can stay here."

"No. No, I don't want to put you out," Lindsay said.

"It's not an imposition. I insist," he said. "It's your only choice."

"Are you sure?"

"Yeah," he said. "You can stay in the loft on the third floor. It has a private bath."

She appeared relieved. "Okay, thank you so much."

Axel ventured outside into the rain to get Lindsay's luggage from her car. It looked like she did indeed have all her belongings inside. She hadn't exaggerated her dire situation. Once he got her settled in the loft, Axel returned to the main floor and paced. He didn't want to be here with Lindsay. Jogging into his room, Axel opened the large chest and stuffed a change of clothes and his toothbrush into an overnight bag.

Just as Lindsay had sought shelter at his place, he needed a different kind of shelter—and he was willing to brave a hurricane in order to get it. Hopefully, he would be welcomed and not turned away.

Chapter Seventeen

Maddie had almost fallen asleep when she heard the banging. She should leave him outside. Because only a nincompoop would be knocking on her door in the middle of a hurricane watch. From the other side of the door, Maddie could hear the whistle of the wind competing with the thunder. She kept a firm grip on her front door and cracked it open a smidgen to let Axel inside.

He was soaking wet.

"What are you doing here in this weather?"

"I couldn't stay there" was all he said before dropping his duffel bag on her living room floor.

"Did you lose power?" she asked.

"No."

"Did a tree hit your house?"

"No."

She released an exasperated breath. "Then why are you here?"

"I had an unexpected guest," Axel said, taking off his shirt. "Lindsay showed up, and I had to give her a place to stay."

Maddie had a huge problem with that explanation. "Why is Lindsay spending the night in your house?" Her tone sounded as harsh as she felt.

He tugged his pants down while he filled her in. Maddie did her best to listen while trying not to be distracted by the man undressing before her. Most of his clothes were now in a damp puddle at his feet, and he stood before her in his boxers. She dashed to the linen closet to get him an oversize towel. Axel thanked her and proceeded to dry off his body. She watched him rub the towel over his torso before moving lower. All he needed to do was gyrate his hips and she would be in the middle of a striptease.

Maddie turned around and wiped her brow.

The man was a walking erotic fantasy. Tonight was going to be a restless night.

"So, she intrudes in your space, and your response is to invade mine," she said.

"I don't know her like I know you," Axel said. "Plus, I can't have the media seeing her there and getting the wrong idea."

That heedless statement pushed her button. She spun to face him, her left eye ticking. "Do you know how insulting you sound right now? So, your being here with me is safe because I'm a plain Jane?"

His eyes went wide. "I didn't mean that..." He stammered. "I'm comfortable with you. I don't see you that way."

"What way?" she huffed out. "I have a good mind to toss you out to deal with Hurricane Shelley's fury, because she's no match for my anger right now."

Axel stepped close with the towel wrapped about his waist. She kept her gaze on his face to keep from ogling his well-defined chest, but there was nothing she could do to stop her own chest from heaving.

"You want to know how I see you?" Axel cupped her head in his hands. "I see you as a friend." His voice dropped. "I trust you. When I'm in your presence, I feel empowered. I feel like as long as you're in my corner, I can conquer anything. Trust me when I say you're no plain Jane. You are exquisite. Remarkable. And to borrow a line from *Aladdin*, a diamond in the rough."

Her breath caught. *Well, dang.*

She touched her chest and licked her lips. His eyes followed her movement. He moved a hand to stroke her face. "Where's Keri?" he asked.

"She's in Mexico," Maddie breathed out. Her voice didn't sound like her own. She sounded raspy, throaty. Thirsty.

"Oh" was all he said, that one word holding sultry promise, before he stepped farther into her personal space. Daring her. Challenging her. She put a hand on Axel's chest, intending to push him away or stop him from getting too close.

That was a mistake. Electricity sizzled where her palm made contact with his body.

Awareness surged, crackling between them.

Then there was nothing but heat. But she shivered, remembering she was braless and dressed in a sheer nightgown. Axel noticed. His eyes darkened, and he tucked a finger under her chin to lift it, to angle it, just so. He used his other hand to trace the outline of her lips. Then he hugged her close and rocked.

"Being in your arms is like home," he whispered in her ear. "I could hold you like this forever." His voice caused thrills to reverberate through her body. Axel pressed his lips against her ear, feathery light, as if he were testing to see her reaction.

She wrapped her hands around his waist and moaned. That was all the encouragement Axel needed, tightening his hold. He threaded his fingers through her hair and inhaled. "Your hair always smells like some kind of citrus, and it always drives me nuts."

Always? Interesting…

Emboldened, Maddie lowered her hands to cup his butt. Nice. Firm. The towel fell to the floor and she could feel the evidence of his desire. Axel groaned in her ear.

"Baby, you're going to make me do things you're not ready for."

"Speak for yourself."

He chuckled. "That's my girl. You always give as good as you get—speak your mind," he said, running his hands down her back. Everywhere he touched ignited a fire, a yearning.

"We've never crossed the professional line, but you're leaving in a few days."

"Yes, I am."

"That changes things," he said, his voice holding promise.

Goodness. Would he just kiss her already?

"If that's what you want," he said, rocking his hips, his voice eager. "There's no reason why we can't have fun. Blur the lines a little."

"Did I say that comment about kissing me aloud?"

Axel chuckled and kissed her neck. "Yes. You did. I'll get there, but I'm still in disbelief that you're letting me hug you like this." His lips moved across her collarbone. Goose bumps followed his path. And desire. And impatience.

Enough was enough.

Maddie grabbed Axel's head and pressed her lips to his. In that instant, Axel took charge, his tongue demanding she give him entrance. Maddie was happy to oblige, her eyes closing of their own volition. He filled her space, kissing her long and hard, with skill, with precision, like he had no intention of ever stopping.

And his hands. Oh, his hands.

They were everywhere, discovering her, like they were memorizing every inch of her body.

And still he kissed her, barely allowing her to get any air. Relentless, like he had to taste every drop of what she had to offer.

And Maddie let him.

Because—

Just…because.

Then Axel did something amazing. He hummed into her mouth. Hummed the words to her favorite song while his tongue continued its exploration. And she was putty. And she was humming right along with him. Their bodies swaying to the rhythm, creating their own tempo.

Then finally, mercifully, he ended the kiss and let her go.

Maddie opened her eyes and touched her lips, scorched with passion. "I'm not going to sleep with you," she croaked out, denying the ripples of desire slaking through her being.

"I know. You're not ready," he said. "Besides, I need to recover." Those words pleased her immensely. Then he tilted his head. "How did it feel to kiss me? Axel the man, not the actor, not the superhero."

She saw a vulnerability reflected in his eyes and realized this wasn't a roundabout way to get a compliment on his skills. Axel needed to know she hadn't sought the fantasy and that everything they had just shared was solely about him.

So, she decided to be honest. As she always was. As he needed. She took a moment to gather her thoughts and then attempted to express what she had experienced into words. "Kissing you was an out-of-body, mind-numbing escapade. I've never experienced anything like it, and when I'm in bed tonight, I intend to replay that kiss in my mind over and over again."

Then she exhaled.

Chapter Eighteen

"You need to tell her before it hits social media," Caleb said, his voice barely above a whisper.

"I completely agree," Lynx said, stretching his legs out in front of him.

It was two days after the hurricane threat and *that* kiss. A kiss from which he still felt the aftereffects. It had taken the strength of Hercules to keep his hands and mouth off Maddie. So, he hadn't bothered to try. Every chance he got, Axel made sure his lips were pressed against hers. In the hallway, at her door, by her car. If they were alone and away from prying eyes, their lips locked. He sought to replicate that moment, and he wasn't disappointed. Each time was sweeter and sweeter than before.

It was like he was fifteen again, enthralled with

his first kiss. It was exhilarating. Of course, as he, Lynx and Caleb sat fishing right before daybreak, Axel didn't portray it like that. He tried to be cool in the retelling, simply saying he had gotten to first base and was worried about how Maddie would react when she heard about his next gig. And the fact that he was going to miss the school play.

After attaching a shrimp to his hook, Axel tossed his line. "I know, but things are good with us right now. I don't want to ruin that."

Lynx shook his head, his dark hair falling in his face. Swooping it back with his free hand, he said, "You don't know what she'll say. You can't assume to know her reaction. Not telling her is a certain way to ruin things." He pulled his line in and reached for one of Axel's shrimp.

"You're right," Axel said.

"Tell me something I don't know."

Caleb grinned, tucking his cap low on his head. "Lynx has become the expert on women ever since he and Shanna got engaged. Everything is Shanna, Shanna, Shanna."

Lynx gave his brother a light shove. "Whatever. Just wait until you get engaged or fall in love. You'll see." He snorted. "You're going to be the most lovesick of all."

Lifting a hand, Caleb said, "I'm good. I'm not getting bitten by the love bug, ever. You can keep that disease to yourself. Watching you and Shanna makes me queasy."

Axel's mouth quirked in a grin. Lynx was more

than in love—he was besotted. Axel was happy for him, but like Caleb, he didn't want love to have him acting a fool. Sure, he and Maddie were having fun, but that was all it would be.

Nevertheless, he defended his brother. "I wouldn't say it's sickening." That was the best he could do.

Caleb slanted a gaze Axel's way and opened his mouth like he was about to shift the focus to Axel's escapades with Maddie. "You two need to quit it," Axel said to divert him. "We're here to fish."

Jutting his jaw at Axel, Caleb said, "You're next. In fact, I would say you've already been bitten and the virus is taking over your system. You've already begun displaying symptoms."

Lynx cracked up. "Caleb, you really know how to beat a metaphor to death."

Axel felt a tug on his line and stood. "I've got something."

"You can't be serious!" Caleb exclaimed, lifting his own line to investigate. His hook was empty. The worm he had attached must have fallen off. Again.

His younger brother was stubborn. Axel had told him to use shrimp, but Caleb didn't want to waste his worms. They had cost him a couple bucks, and he was going to get a return on his investment.

The fish on Axel's line was fighting for its freedom. He tightened his grip and reeled it in. It was a bass and a good nine pounds from the looks of it. "Look at that beauty," he yelled.

He and Lynx high-fived. Each of them had caught about three fish. Caleb hadn't been as lucky.

Caleb helped him unhook the fish and snapped a picture. Then Axel threw it back into the river.

"Why did you do that?" Caleb asked. "That one was big enough to feed all three of us."

Axel shrugged. "Fish are like women. They both like to be free."

Lynx rolled his eyes. "Please tell me that's not a line from one of your movies."

"As a matter of fact, it is," Axel said, lowering his cap over his eyes. The sun was already out, and he had forgotten his shades at home.

"I don't know how you make millions with such corny lines," Caleb said.

"Don't hate. Appreciate."

"Whatever, bro."

Axel returned to the discussion of telling Maddie about his upcoming movie. "I'll tell Maddie after the *Mantis* premiere."

"Make sure," Caleb warned.

"I think you're procrastinating because you know she's going to be disappointed—and the students will, too. The fact that you're talking about it is a sign. You should tell her today," Lynx warned.

The men returned to shore and anchored the boat on the trailer attached to Caleb's truck. It was a decent-size boat that Caleb had built with his own hands. One of his brother's do-it-yourself projects. Axel had offered many times to give him an upgrade, but Caleb loved his boat. He said all the dings and scratches gave it character.

"I had a good time with you turkeys," Axel said. "It's good being home with family."

"This was like the old days," Caleb said. "Except this time I didn't get tossed in the lake with the gators." It was common knowledge in Florida that anywhere there was a body of water, there were sure to be alligators, so Caleb wasn't exaggerating.

After a quick huddle, the brothers parted ways. Lynx had taken the day to scout wedding venues with Shanna and do some cake testing. To Axel, that sounded like a chore, mundane, but Lynx was just as excited as his wife-to-be.

Axel headed home and took a quick shower before heading over to the school. He spotted Maddie's car immediately, and his heart rate escalated. He couldn't wait to see her, though it had only been a few hours since he had last seen her.

Yes, he had it that bad, and he would wear it on a T-shirt. He just wasn't going to confirm his brothers' suspicions.

Lindsay was waiting for him outside.

"Did you check out the hotel I reserved for you?" he asked.

She fell in line with him, clipboard in hand. "Yes, it's spacious and wonderful. Although I did forget your code name. It took me a minute to remember to ask for Artemis Fall."

"Good, good."

"Is there anything you need me to do?" she asked.

They entered the door that led directly to the auditorium. "No. No. Maddie's got it handled." His eyes searched for Maddie, trying to spot her curls.

She lifted her shoulders. "Axel, you hired me to assist. I need the chance to do so."

"Isn't she training you?"

"Yes, but she won't let me handle the major stuff. Like your upcoming premiere. Maddie insists on overseeing that trip herself. I'm more than capable of handling your needs. Especially since she's leaving."

Axel paused and shifted his attention to Lindsay. She appeared to be earnest, and she was right about Maddie's departure. Not that he wanted to think about that. "Maddie knows me. I'm sure you know about the backlash I faced on social media. This trip back home was a hiatus, a chance for the brouhaha to die down. The premiere will be my first venture back into my world."

"That's why, as your assistant, I should be going with you."

Axel jutted his jaw. Was she trying to argue with him? But then again, wasn't that what he wanted? He gestured for Lindsay to continue.

"Attending the premiere is the hands-on experience I need. I need to watch Maddie in action so I can take notes."

She had a point. Axel couldn't fault her for wanting to do a good job. Particularly since he would be the one to benefit. The bell rang, and Axel was eager to get to the students.

He made a rash decision. "All right. You've convinced me. Have Maddie set it up."

"Okay, great." Lindsay made a move to leave but then whipped around. "There's one more thing."

"What is it?" he asked, his patience strained.

"I'll need a dress. I don't want to embarrass you."

He tapped his feet. "Maddie can get you hooked up with a stylist. Anything else?"

"No. Thanks," she said, her eyes shining. "I'll make you proud."

"I'm sure." Axel headed to the front of the auditorium and went up to the stage. He called for the students to huddle around. He searched for Maddie but didn't see her. She must have gone into the prop room. Maddie was good with a sewing machine and had hemmed a few of the costumes.

"You all have been working real hard—giving one hundred and ten percent—and I just want to say I'm proud of you. I wanted to let you know that I've purchased a new stage and lighting system and a better set for *The Sound of Music*. This will be done over the weekend. So, when you return on Monday, you'll see a big difference."

"Woot! Woot!" the students hollered.

Maddie returned, holding a couple of the dresses in her hands. Lindsay followed behind. Maddie avoided his gaze and flounced past the students with a forced cheerfulness. Then Lindsay appeared from the back, her chin lifted, her face triumphant. Axel could almost smell the scent of the match, the kindling, and somehow he knew he had started a fire. Maddie was furious with him, though she was putting on a good act. He was in tune enough with her to know that, but Axel had no idea what he had done wrong. He did know Lindsay was involved and vowed to ask her about it.

After rehearsal, Maddie stormed through the exit with the force of a tornado, so he couldn't confront her.

Lindsay hovered behind to assist. He posed the question with a careful, light tone. "Did something happen with you and Maddie?"

The young woman tilted her head. "No. Why do you ask?"

"Are you sure?"

She shrugged. "I have no idea. Maddie is…driven. I only told her that you told me to check with her about getting my hair styled, makeup and outfit for the premiere. She twisted her lips and nodded. But she didn't say anything else about it. Just asked me to help her carry the costumes."

"I see." Axel knew then that Maddie had a problem with Lindsay attending. He wasn't sure why, because Maddie had attended events with him in the past as his assistant. He was only planning to do the same with Lindsay… Unless, she saw it as more? Like a date?

No. Maddie was too practical for that. She knew they were having some adult playtime. Axel's plan was to keep things fun between them, lighthearted. Their lip-locking sessions were something he could reminisce and smile about, and he hoped she would as well. Because in a matter of days, they would be going their separate ways.

Although Axel was anticipating going to the premiere with Maddie by his side. It would be sentimental for him—their last formal event together. Maddie could relax and delegate all her usual tasks to Lindsay. It all seemed really simple and straightforward in his mind. He would stop by Maddie's and explain all this to her. She would understand and appreciate his reasoning.

But then, before he left, Lindsay cornered him. "What will you be wearing to the premiere? I want to make sure we're color coordinated."

"That's not necessary," Axel said in a crisp, firm tone, finding her request odd. Like she was getting too familiar, too soon. Maybe she meant no harm, but Axel didn't want any confusion between them. She was beautiful, but he wasn't attracted to her. Not even a tiny speck of interest buzzed within him.

She gave an awkward laugh. "You're right. I guess you could say I was doing too much. That would be extra."

"Yes. I would say that, and it would be, as you say, extra."

Her mouth popped open. "Whoa. I guess you told me." An even more awkward laugh.

Well, if she was going to work for him, Lindsay would need to know he wasn't a pushover. Or clueless when it came to women. In fact, he knew with ambitious women like Lindsay, it was best to be frank.

He looked her square in the eyes, seeing her practiced innocence. He folded his arms. "Lindsay, I think you're cool, and we click. That's part of the reason

I hired you, but we're not cool like that. You get my drift? I'm being very clear where the lines are, because I don't want any problems between us."

Her eyes went wide before she gave a meek nod and whispered, "Whatever you say, boss."

Chapter Nineteen

Speed walking around the pond at the park near her condo, Maddie ignored Axel's call, annoyed to even see his name pop up on her phone. She didn't have a reason to be irritated that he'd invited Lindsay along to the premiere—could even understand his rationale. But Lindsay had sashayed into the prop room, demanding Maddie relinquish her access to Axel's charge accounts.

Oh, her tone had been sweet, but Lindsay reminded Maddie of what her Jamaican father would call a green lizard, changing its color overnight. Maddie could only hope she was wrong, or that Axel would set Lindsay straight, because Maddie wasn't letting go until the last possible minute.

She released a plume of air and began a second

lap around the park. Her judgment could be clouded by a green monster chomping away at her insides. Because when Lindsay had announced that she was going to the premiere and would be overseeing all Axel's needs, Maddie had had to squelch the unexpected jealousy. She wanted to shout that she would take care of Axel. But she had clamped her jaw to keep from lashing out. Even now, thinking about it made her chest heave.

It was childish, but Maddie wanted to hit something. Or someone. Like Axel. Forget about being reasonable. Why would he invite Lindsay to their last event together? She knew it was business related, but it was also personal. A sort-of date.

Maddie stopped. Maybe that was the problem. She was making more of things between them than she should. Or, rather, than Axel did. He had made it clear before his lips touched hers that they were only having fun.

She resumed walking and picked up her pace. Maybe she could sweat this man out of her system, because he had invaded her head space. Her mind was full of him. He was the first person she wanted to see and the last she wanted to talk to before she went to sleep. That truth made her stop once again. She made her way to the edge of the pond, searching for her duck.

She didn't see it. Maybe it had moved on to bigger things, like she would. That's why it made no sense to be mad with Lindsay. She squared her shoulders. Tomorrow, Maddie would open a line of credit for

Lindsay with a set limit. Axel could expand it further when he decided. Or when she had earned his trust. However, as his current assistant, Maddie needed to look out for his interests. A part of that did mean training Lindsay on handling a big event. Before she could change her mind, Maddie called Lindsay.

"Can you pick up Axel's suit at the cleaner's? I dropped it off to get it steam pressed yesterday. And, I'll need you to order some big-ticket items from Joni's baby registry on Axel's behalf. Joni is Axel's publicist," she supplied in case Lindsay wasn't aware.

"Sure thing. I can do that. Do you want me to drop the suit off at his house?" she asked in a deferential tone, sounding a little…deflated and a lot less cocky. Maddie wondered about the change but didn't question it. She had given Lindsay a spare key to Axel's home.

"Yes, that would be great. I'll text you the address to the cleaner's and the link to the registry. See you tomorrow."

With that task delegated, Maddie picked her way across the path, passing the children at the playground. She squinted, seeing a tall, familiar figure pushing a little girl on a swing. He was in deep conversation with another man, who she assumed to be the girl's father. Maddie meandered through the playground equipment until she was a few feet away.

It was Axel. Chatting it up with a fan. The man appeared to be in awe, snapping pictures of Axel while his daughter squealed with delight.

She stuffed her hands in the pockets of her dress

and watched him. She knew he had spotted her, because he gave a little wave. She waved back. A few minutes later, Axel and the man posed for a selfie before Axel sauntered over to where she stood.

"What are you doing here?" she asked.

"Why didn't you answer my call?" he asked instead of answering.

"I asked a question first." She commenced walking back down the path. She would retrace her steps to the pond.

"I was looking for you. What else?" he said, sounding exasperated, and followed after her. He slowed his strides to match hers. "You weren't answering your cell, so I went to your condo. Your car was there and I rang the doorbell. When you didn't answer, I decided to come to the park. I know you like to come here and think."

She rolled her eyes. He knew her habits well. "That's why I didn't answer. I needed some think time. Why were you looking for me?"

They walked in synchrony. "When you left today, I know you were upset." He gave her a playful shove. "I had to investigate. I don't want my favorite girl mad at me."

Maddie wouldn't deny that she had been upset. She wasn't going to volunteer the full truth, though. "I wished you had let me know about Lindsay going to the premiere instead of sending her to tell me. She caught me off guard. That's all."

"You sure?" he quizzed.

She slid a glance his way. "I guess I didn't realize

how much I'm going to miss working for you. Lindsay is ready to take over, but I don't know if I'm ready to hand over the reins."

"I get that, but being with me is holding you back."

She placed a hand on his arm. "I don't regret my time with you. Not one minute. You're a generous boss, and I love how close you are with your family."

Axel stopped. He turned her to face him. "Madison Henry, I enjoy you. You're spunky and fun. My family thinks you're an angel for putting up with me. I like to think I have prepared you to deal with men like Artie. If you think I'm high-maintenance, wait until you start working with him."

Maddie chuckled. "After you, he'll be a piece of cake."

Axel touched her face for a brief second and grew serious. "I have something I'd like to ask you."

She tilted her head. "Go ahead."

"What color dress are you wearing to the premiere?" He looked down at his sneakers with sudden interest, swishing his foot back and forth on the pavement.

"I'm wearing royal blue," she said, her heart thundering in her chest. There was only one reason he would be asking, but she warned herself not to draw conclusions from his question.

"That's a great color for you," he said. Then he lowered his eyes. "I think I'll wear something to match you. If you think that's a good idea."

Was Axel Harrington being shy? Maddie's heart

melted. He was adorable. Sexy as ever. But very much adorable.

"I'd like that very much," she breathed out.

Axel's head shot up, and then he smiled. He puffed his chest and took her hand. Giving her a tug, he started a light jog. "All right then. It's a date. Uh, well, you know what I mean." He was back to being his cocky self.

Maddie couldn't hold back her smile. To see Axel a little nervous and unsure did wonders for her ego. They stood by the pond talking until near sunset. When Maddie started swatting at mosquitoes, they knew it was time to go. Neither one was wearing bug spray, and the Florida mosquitoes grew fat over exposed skin.

Challenging him to a race, Maddie shot past him and sped down the path. She could hear him behind her and pushed her legs faster, mindful not to twist her ankle. Of course, Axel moved in front of her with ease, even jogging backward, taunting her to catch up to him until they were back in her condo parking lot. He gave her a peck on the cheek before taking her hand. She slipped her hand in his, treasuring the security she felt.

She was going to miss this man. More than she could ever admit to him.

Seeing a black stretch limousine, Maddie slowed. The windows were tinted so you couldn't see who was inside. But Maddie had a suspicion. No one used limos anymore…except Faran. Her stomach knotted.

"I wonder who's inside," Axel said, waggling his eyebrows.

Maddie suddenly wanted him gone. Her heart raced, and it had nothing to do with the gorgeous man a few feet from her. The driver opened the door, and a long, lean leg stuck one foot out before a hand extended. The driver took the hand, and her mother stepped out.

Axel pointed, his eyes bulging. He looked at Maddie. "Oh, snap. Do you know who that is?" For once, he sounded awestruck. "That's Faran. I had the biggest crush on her when I was a kid. Then again, so did every man on the planet. What is she doing here?"

That made Maddie's insides twist. "Yes, I know who that is," she said in a dull tone. She hovered behind Axel, hoping her mother hadn't seen her. But that was foolish, because why else would Faran get out of the cool limousine to stand in the heat? She had to have seen Maddie.

"Let's go say hello," Axel said.

Maddie dragged her feet. "I'm hot and sweaty." She had planned to be showered and dressed before her mother arrived. But she had gotten caught up with Axel and had forgotten. Now Faran looked regal, every inch the supermodel, while she looked like she had been rolling in the grass.

But her mother didn't care. She opened her arms and grinned when Maddie drew close.

Axel scrunched his nose. "Does she recognize me?"

Despite feeling frumpy, Maddie chuckled. "She

knows you, but I don't think she expects you to embrace her."

"Maddie, darling. I've been waiting for you." Faran shimmied.

She felt Axel's eyes on her and, from her peripheral vision, saw when his mouth dropped. "You know her?" he asked.

Maddie went to hug her mother, loving the smell of White Diamonds, Faran's favorite perfume. She tightened her grip, squeezing her eyes shut to stem the sudden tears. Maddie hadn't realized how much she had missed her mother until now. After several moments, she pulled away reluctantly.

"I missed you," Faran said, her eyes glossy. "When you called, you knew I had to come. Heidi was nice enough to allow me to use her private jet." She held out a hand to Axel.

Maddie wished she could capture the look on his face. His mouth was opening and closing like a puffer fish.

"It's good to finally meet you. I've heard so much about you." Faran said. She and Axel shook hands, but then Faran began to direct the driver to get her bags. She planned to stay only a few days, but there had to be about five suitcases if Maddie counted correctly.

Axel's eyes darted between them, his confusion evident. "It's good meeting you, too… I'm sorry. How do you two know each other? And, by Heidi, do you mean Heidi Klum?" When Faran nodded, Axel held his head with his hands. "This is my lucky day."

Maddie bit back her laughter. It was good to see

Axel lose his cool. She cleared her throat and delivered the words that made Axel's mouth drop and his eyes widen with disbelief. "Axel, I'd like you to meet my mother, Faran Pigmund, or as she's known to the world—Faran."

Chapter Twenty

Pigmund? Her last name was Pigmund? No wonder Faran had dropped her last name, Axel mused.
"Pigmund." He spoke her surname aloud as he drove
home, testing it out on his tongue. Nope.

Axel had declined their dinner invitation—not
wanting to interrupt the mother-daughter reunion—
and left after helping the driver tote Faran's luggage
into Maddie's condo. He couldn't picture the supermodel being at home in Maddie's small space, much
less her spare room. But Faran hadn't seemed concerned.

In fact, she seemed down-to-earth and every inch
the mother who missed her child.

Why hadn't Maddie told him before? That was the
biggest question on his mind.

Faran. *Faran*, though. Wait until he told his brothers, especially Brigg and Ethan. They were going to be stoked and insist on heading over to Maddie's. No. He wouldn't tell them or they would be pests. As a celebrity, Axel treasured his time with family because he could just be. He didn't have to be on all the time. He couldn't take that away from Faran.

But he would call his parents. Patrick was an even bigger fan. His father wouldn't speak to him if he kept this to himself. Axel called his father and broke the news. His father yelled out to his mother to listen in on the call.

"How long is she here? Do you think she would be up to visitors?" Patrick asked.

"Do you think she would accept a dinner invitation?" Tanya wanted to know.

"I don't know, but she brought enough bags to stay for months," Axel said. "I'll ask Maddie." An idea occurred. "Maybe she can visit with you when Maddie and I go to the premiere. I don't think she's coming with us. Or maybe she is. Why don't you and Mom come with us to Los Angeles? I can get some tickets."

"Yes. That would be good. We could use a weekend away," Patrick said.

"I have to get a dress," Tanya said.

"Why don't you go shopping with Maddie and Faran?" Axel suggested.

"Yeah," Tanya said. "We can make it a girls' day."

"All right. Let me call Maddie and see what can be done."

"I have to get a haircut," Patrick said.

"I need a trim and color, too," Tanya chimed in.

Axel cracked up. "You two are acting like you've never been around celebrities. You've been to events with Hawk and me, rubbed shoulders with many famous faces, so this is so funny to me." Never mind that he had freaked out as well when he had met Faran.

"You sound just as eager as we are," Patrick said. "Admit it. Faran is reclusive. She hasn't made an appearance in the US in years. So, yes, we are really excited."

"All right, I'll let you know."

Axel ended the call and pulled into his driveway. As soon as he put the car in Park, he texted Maddie and with much impatience watched the three dots signaling she was responding. When her text came through, he pumped his fist. Maddie said her mother would love to go to the premiere and to meet his parents and that she would take care of the arrangements. Maddie and Faran welcomed Tanya going dress shopping with them, as well. Before exiting his vehicle, Axel called his parents to give them the update. To say they were ecstatic would be an understatement.

One good thing about her coming was that a Faran sighting would trump his stand-off with Natasha. Thinking of Natasha and that whole debacle, Axel marveled. That felt so long ago, though it had only been weeks. Being home lessened its sting, though it still had relevance when it came to his career.

Fortunately, it hadn't hurt ticket sales. In fact, Joni reported that the scandal only seemed to fuel the sales. Online presales had prompted many theaters to add midnight screenings. Axel was encouraged by that.

Axel entered his home and saw that his suit had been delivered. Lindsay must have dropped it off. It was a navy blue Louis Vuitton suit, perfectly tailored to fit his body. He texted Lindsay to call the designer, and ask him to change the gray shirt to a white one. Since the event was two days away, on Saturday, he would switch out when he arrived to LA.

It was after hours, but Axel made a call to Tiffany and requested jewelry on loan for all three women to accent their dresses. His cell phone alarm sounded, reminding him that he had something important to do. He considered asking Lindsay to handle the task but shook his head. This needed to be personal. From him. He sauntered into his office and got on the computer. It took some searching and clicking, and so many times he wanted to reach out to Maddie, but he persisted. Eventually, Axel found the perfect gift for Maddie.

When he finished placing the order, Axel stretched and yawned. It was too early for bed, but he was so ready for a shower. Stripping and tossing his clothes to the floor, Axel stepped into the massive walk-in shower. Turning on the heat, he allowed the water to beat on his back, soothing the knots in his neck. He hadn't gotten a chance to kiss Maddie this evening before leaving her house.

After drying off and slipping on a pair of blue-striped pajama pants, Axel walked barefooted into his bedroom. The king-size bed loomed large and empty. He had a flashback of Maddie huddled under the covers and wished he had stopped his housekeeper from washing his linens.

Axel Harrington, get a grip.

His phone rang, a welcome respite from the silence. It was Ralph. He quickly answered his cell.

"I pitched that script like you asked. Netflix is definitely interested."

Axel whooped. "Whoa. That is great news." He couldn't wait to call Maddie and surprise her. She was going to be elated. And a household name. Her film could rate as high as *Don't Look Up* or *Squid Game*. He could imagine it all. Axel could see a Golden Globe in his future.

"There's more, though," Ralph said, breaking into his musings. "They have another actor in mind to play the lead."

That made his elation free-fall to his toes. "I don't understand."

"That's business for you," Ralph quipped. "They are eager to make an offer to option the film, so talk it over with Maddie and get back to me. As a matter of fact, I could call her if you'd like?"

"No. I'll talk with her." He forced the words out, his mind filled with the fact that they didn't want him. They wanted someone else. An unfamiliar thread of insecurity snaked through his being. "Why didn't they want me?" he felt compelled to ask, to know.

"Because they felt you need more dramatic experience before tackling that role in *A Summer's Dream.*

They are already talking about changing that title, by the way." Ralph's tone was impersonal, which bothered Axel.

His agent didn't understand how much this script meant to him—how much the writer of the script meant to him. It was Maddie's dream for Axel to play Brock—a man with Asperger's, abandoned by his parents, who hid his diagnosis, joined the military as a paramedic and ended up in the mountains of Thailand. There were scenes where it was just him and nature, and scenes where he learned to navigate his way into this new society. But the standout for Axel was when Brock attracted the attention of a woman who betrayed him, robbed him and left him in a forest, naked and afraid. Axel was confident he could bring that character to life and portray him with authenticity.

His mother's suggestion to produce the film himself came back to him. Maybe he needed to start his own production company.

"I'll let you know what Maddie says."

"Okay. The producers are excited to have you onboard. They have already booked your tickets."

His stomach clenched. He would have to tell Maddie this weekend. Then the students on Monday. Those were two conversations he didn't relish having, but he had to. Axel didn't want them hearing the news from anybody but him.

He sighed. After the premiere.

Chapter Twenty-One

"You two looked real chummy yesterday," Faran said, seated on the chaise longue in their five-star hotel suite. They had arrived in Los Angeles early that morning and had slept in until about noon. Axel's parents were in the rooms across from Maddie and her mother, while Axel was in the penthouse on the floor above them.

When Maddie showed Faran the dress she had chosen, Faran had waved it off as too basic and said they would shop in LA.

Faran's idea of shopping was that the stylist would come to them, bringing several dresses from which to choose while they sipped on tropical punch and snacked on finger foods. Maddie had given her color choice of royal blue, Tanya had chosen eggplant and

Faran gold. Maddie found herself excited to see what the stylist would bring.

When Maddie called her mother for assistance with getting ready for the premiere, she had expected her mother to send her pictures or web links. But Faran never did the expected. Her mother had booked her flight, saying she was glad to use this opportunity to spend time with her only child. Faran had also arranged for Maddie to get her hair done in LA, and that would now include Tanya and Faran as well. However, Faran would apply Maddie's makeup herself, and Maddie looked forward to that special treat.

One of the suitcases Faran brought was filled with exotic shoes. Maddie had been delighted. She had her eye on a silver pair to accentuate her gown.

"What do you mean?" Maddie asked, avoiding her mother's gaze and sipping on her punch. She should have known Faran wouldn't let the weekend go by without mentioning it. Tanya hadn't arrived yet, which was why her mother had broached the topic.

"I saw the way you two were holding hands and all that." She crossed her legs and adjusted the bust of her strapless jumper. "Are you two knocking boots?"

Maddie spewed some of her juice on her checkered blouse. Wiping her chin and shirt, she said, "Mom, really? No one says that anymore. Ugh. Not that I want to discuss my personal business with my mother, but, no, we aren't together like that. We're just messing around. Having fun. Geesh. I can't believe you asked me that."

Faran cracked up. "Hey, you didn't have to answer."

Maddie shook her head before going to get herself some more punch. "Who is this and what have you done with my mother? Since when do you talk like this?"

Getting to her feet and gyrating her hips and waving a hand in the air, Faran said, "Your mama was young, too, once. Fifty is the new twenty. I still got it going on."

"Goodness, Mom. Stay off TikTok," Maddie said. "And can you please stop talking like that to me?" She shook her head and gestured between them. "We don't talk like that—at least not to each other. This feels weird. I don't even know what to say. Just behave when Tanya comes."

Faran chuckled and switched to perfect French. *"Si vous l'avez, affichez-le."*

"Let others who have it, flaunt it. Right now, I just want my mom. All right?"

With a nod, Faran settled back onto the chaise longue. "All right, dear. I'll curb my enthusiasm, but this is the first time you've wanted to get dolled up. You refused to go to homecoming or prom, so I'm excited to see you interested in fashion."

Maddie pulled her glasses on her face. "I want to look beautiful, and you're the most beautiful person I know, inside and out."

Faran dabbed at her eyes. "Thank you. You're going to make me ruin my cat eyes."

Tanya arrived, and Maddie grabbed a celery stick before opening the door. Tanya was dressed in a pair of slacks and a floral top. Maddie thought she looked lovely. Holding the celery between her teeth, she greeted the other woman with a hug, then introduced Tanya to her mother.

"It's great meeting you," Tanya said, going to shake Faran's hand. "We all love your daughter so much."

"Believe me when I say the pleasure is mine," Faran said, scooping Tanya into an embrace.

"You're even lovelier in person. Now I see where Maddie gets her beauty."

Maddie snorted but chewed on the celery to keep from uttering a rebuttal. Tanya was sweet, but comparing her to her mother was an exaggeration. She peered at Faran from under her lashes. Hopefully, her mother wouldn't take offense.

But Faran beamed. "Thanks so much. Maddie was her father's spitting image as a child, but I am glad that as she gets older, I see more of me emerge. She's becoming my mini-me—the slightly shorter version."

Maddie's eyes bulged. Wait, what? Besides their eye color, she didn't see a resemblance. But, whatever. Both women were obviously being polite.

To Maddie's delight, Faran and Tanya hit it off, and they were both masters at conversation. In a short time, they covered a range of topics, sounding like they had known each other for years. Maddie was content to listen to their small talk until the stylist arrived.

Pepper was of Asian descent and had the energy of a rocket, wheeling in two racks filled with dresses. Tanya and Faran strolled over to the first rack with their chosen dress colors while Maddie approached the other rack stacked with royal blue gowns with apprehension. She hoped there would be some good choices for her size and curves. But the woman was a genius, because all the gowns seemed made for her in mind. She skimmed through the clothes before one caught her eye. It was a formfitting Louis Vuitton crystal-embellished gown.

Uttering a silent prayer, Maddie went into the other room to try it on. Pepper followed her to assist. The older woman clucked her tongue, adjusting and tucking. But when she was done, Maddie gasped.

She wasn't a duckling. She was a swan. *Swan*tastic. A curvaceous, self-assured woman. Twisting this way and that, Maddie ran her hands down the sides of her hips. She liked how she looked from every vantage point, and she felt like a real-life Cinderella.

"Let's try another," Pepper suggested after snapping Maddie's picture on her phone.

"I'm good with this," Maddie said.

"But you want to be sure," Pepper said in a firm tone, as in, *don't argue with me.* She unzipped the gown and exited the room.

Maddie didn't protest because she didn't think she could, though she dreaded trying on more dresses. So, she waited for Pepper to return with more choices. She carefully stepped out of the gown and placed it on the bed.

Pepper came in, holding two dresses. "I think these will fit nicely." Placing one on the bed, she held up the other. "Let's check this one first."

The design featured a plunging neckline, lantern sleeves, two splits in the front and a tightened bodice at the waist. She wasn't sure about this one. But once it was on, Maddie drew in a deep breath. The dress was stunning and draped her frame in a way that celebrated her curves. She stood with her mouth open, speechless. Pepper snapped a pic with her openmouthed.

"See. What did I tell you?" Pepper grinned, framing Maddie's hair around her face.

Maddie was now eager to give the third choice a try. It was strapless, formfitting with mermaid ruching on the bottom. "I can't believe this," Maddie said, once she had it on. "I don't know which one to wear now." Once again, Pepper took a picture.

"Let's have Faran decide," Pepper said with a knowing smile.

Walking after the other woman, Maddie made sure to keep the dress from touching the ground. When she entered the room, Faran and Tanya stopped talking and gazed. She could see their chosen dresses lying on the bed.

"I love that color against your skin," Faran observed.

"Flawless," Tanya said, cupping her mouth.

Pepper showed them the other two pictures. They oohed and ahhed.

"Aren't they all good?" Maddie said, surprised to find she was having fun. "I don't want to choose just one."

"Then don't. Get them all," Faran said.

Maddie shook her head. "I don't need three gowns in the same color. I just need to decide."

Pepper chimed in, "I can have the other gowns shipped to you in different colors."

Faran clapped her hands. "That would be wonderful."

Maddie's stomach clenched. "I can't have Axel spending all this money for dresses I might never wear."

"Axel would be thrilled," Tanya interjected.

"I'll pick up the tab on the other two," her mother stated.

"I don't know..." Maddie didn't feel right.

"It's one thing to realize your worth, daughter. It's another to accept it."

Her mother's words settled in Maddie's heart. She met Faran's eyes and saw her mother meant them. With a small shrug, Maddie whispered, "Thank you."

"So, which one will you wear today?" Tanya asked.

Maddie sighed. "I'm usually so decisive, but I have no clue." She studied the pictures at length. These gowns weren't for an assistant. Each screamed, "Look at me! See me!" Each made a statement.

Like a mind reader, Faran spoke with quiet impact, serving out some good advice. "Whenever you're in doubt, go with what feels right. Why blend in when you can stand out?"

Chapter Twenty-Two

She wore white.

A not-so-subtle jab. Her publicist was a genius. Natasha stood a few feet ahead of him, dressed in a floor-length slip dress, smiling and posing for the media. The throng of onlookers screamed her name. She had a small entourage behind her.

Axel had arrived a few minutes after 4:30 p.m. with Lindsay and his parents. He had retained two bodyguards—at Maddie's insistence—for this trip and reserved two SUVs at the airport. The men had traveled with him from Florida to LA. Faran would make her own entrance with Maddie a little closer to five. The movie would begin at five thirty. Axel hadn't minded, stifling his minor disappointment that Maddie wasn't traveling with him. This wasn't a date, after all. Though his mother must not think so. She had sent him several texts:

Wait until you see Maddie

and:

Maddie's going to knock your socks off!

Which must be the reason why he felt this eagerness to see her.

He had added a blue handkerchief and cuffs as accents to coordinate with her royal blue dress.

The scent of popcorn teased his nostrils. Axel had had a light breakfast but hadn't eaten since because he didn't want to chance a stomachache. However, he intended to have a small bag of the popcorn along with some finger food. Nothing too heavy. Maddie had made reservations at the APL Restaurant on Vine Street for 8:30 p.m. and he planned to make up for his missed meal with the rib eye.

"This is exciting, isn't it?" Lindsay whispered, tagging behind him. She had dressed in a simple, form-fitting green minidress with gold sandals. Her VIP access pass hung around her neck on a jeweled lanyard.

Ignoring the flashing cameras, Axel nodded. He had forgotten what it was like for a newbie to this life. She had stars in her eyes, but Axel had warned her not to approach any other celebrities. "Yes, but remember most of what you see here is a mirage," he said, keeping his smile firmly in place.

"Hey, Axel, can we get a shot?" a reporter yelled.

With a practiced grin, Axel posed with his parents flanking him. After which his parents decided to head to the VIP room, and Axel made his way toward Natasha, who had stopped to talk to BET. Joni had already cleared it with Natasha's publicist, who had finally responded. They'd arranged for the actors to take two shots together. Two. One on the red carpet and the other following the movie.

"Wait here," he said to Lindsay and meandered his way through the crowd until he was in Natasha's view.

Moving behind her, Axel placed an arm around her waist, saying hello and giving her an air kiss to the cheek. She tensed beneath his touch, but like the professional she was, the smile she projected for the press was warm. They took the first picture with her body curved into his, saying to the world that all was forgiven, all was well.

They both knew the truth.

He had been given every step to take. He had been warned not to maintain physical contact once the photo was snapped. Axel was eager to put this scandal behind them—hopefully since Natasha had agreed, she felt the same. So he removed his arm, gave her a friendly wave and then pressed on. Then he released the breath he hadn't realized he had been holding. That had gone exactly as outlined and agreed.

He resisted the urge to wipe his brow, because he knew the media was studying his movements with the precision of eagles, hoping, waiting for him to make a wrong move.

Axel gestured to Lindsay to join him. "You can go ahead and secure our seats, enjoy a snack in the VIP lounge if you'd like. I still have to mingle a bit."

She nodded, giddy with excitement, and took off.

Axel spotted the director, Nico Washington, and went over and greeted him. The men hugged, thumping each other on the back, and then posed for the press. "You know the producers would like to do a part two, right?" Nico said.

"Let's see how this does," Axel hedged. Call him paranoid, but he was convinced some of the reporters were lip-readers, and even if they weren't, there were microphones everywhere. "We'll talk soon."

"All right. Here's to rave reviews tonight," Nico said before they bumped fists. He turned to wave at the crowd before going inside the auditorium.

Once inside the VIP lounge, Axel grabbed two small plates and piled on the finger foods. He was saving one for Maddie. He had just made his way through the line when he heard a low whistle. He turned to see what was going on and stopped still.

Faran had entered. She was ethereal in sheer gold. Photographers rushed to immortalize her regal pose, and like the queen she was, Faran gave a small hint of her signature smile. Axel tilted his head, searching the crowd, knowing Maddie wouldn't be too far behind.

A woman dressed in a stunning royal blue gown and a pair of unusual silver shoes wove her way through the crowd, drawing the eyes of onlookers. Axel wondered if she was a new actress or a singer.

Either way, she was captivating. He loved how the dress flowed when she walked, revealing two hidden slits in the front, which allowed a glimpse of smooth, shapely legs. Her hair was pinned in a messy high bun. He started when he realized she was making her way toward him, lifting a hand in greeting.

It wasn't until the stranger was a few inches away, when he identified those remarkable eyes, that Axel recognized the vision before him. "Maddie?" he asked, not able to hide his astonishment. "You're not wearing your glasses." He knew he had stated the obvious, but he was in shock.

"Ever heard of contacts?" She laughed, her voice throaty, her kissable neck exposed.

A camera flash made him remember that he was at his premiere event with thousands scrutinizing his every action—although Faran mostly commanded their attention right now. Axel led Maddie into one of the VIP rooms to give them a measure of privacy.

"What did you do to your hair?" He sounded daft, but again, he blamed his odd behavior on amazement. "I got you a plate," he added.

Maddie touched her updo, careful not to mess with her beaded crown and asked, "Do you like it?"

"Like it? I love it. And whoever did your makeup has some serious skills. You look like you, but flaw-less." He appreciated the purple tint on Maddie's full lips. He would love sucking it off her lips later.

Her eyes sparkled. "My mom did it," she said, touching her lips briefly and appearing uncomfortable.

"To put it in a word, you are a vision." He eyed

the Tiffany chandelier earrings dangling from her ears. He couldn't stop staring. "I could look at you all night."

"Thank you, but I'm still me," Maddie said, with attitude. "It's just a dress and makeup, Axel, which makes up less than one percent of my life. The rest of the time, I'm just me. Simply Maddie."

Axel wasn't sure why Maddie seemed to be upset at his praise, but his eyes feasted on her, appreciating her transformation. "I vote that you never wear glasses again. Those eyes are too spectacular to hide behind your dorky frames."

"Dorky?" She poked him in the chest. "Snap out of it, Axel. This isn't a scene from *Cinderella* where all the magic ends at midnight and I'm left holding a glass shoe. When I get home tonight, I'm going to have real blisters from these heels I had to wear just to enhance this dress." She shook her head.

He lifted her hand and pressed his lips to her wrist. "I don't know how I'm going to keep my hands off you tonight."

She yanked her hand away. "The same way you've resisted me for years, that's how. I can't with you." In a flash she left him standing there, mouth agape. Axel shook his head. He had never had a woman furious with him because he complimented her. But one guarantee when it came to Maddie was that she would always do the unexpected.

Yet another woman was about to surprise him.

He exited the VIP room holding both plates in his hand, looking for Maddie, when he almost bumped into Natasha. She had been about to enter the food line and took one of the plates out of his hand.

"Thanks, I didn't eat all morning," she said, picking up a carrot stick to crunch on it.

Axel took a bite of a chicken tender, wondering why Natasha was talking to him. "There's no press around at the moment, so you don't have to play nice."

"I'm not playing nice," she said, running her eyes across his body. "It looks like you came alone."

"I brought my parents."

"I came by myself, but I was hoping not to leave by myself." Her tone was both seductive and suggestive.

His eyes narrowed. "What are you up to?" They both had stopped eating at that point.

"Axel, I wanted to say I'm sorry. I shouldn't have tried to corner you into an engagement."

From the corner of his right eye, Axel could see Maddie approaching. Again, she had admirers scoping her out, but she was oblivious. Knowing her, she had calmed down and was coming to get her food. He needed Natasha to go on her way. "Thanks for saying that, Natasha. But let's move forward."

She sidled closer to him and whispered, "I want you back."

"You couldn't have called?" Axel shot back. "You wait for situations like these when there are others around to get me to agree with you." Maddie was now within earshot. He groaned on the inside.

"I'm not being manipulative," Natasha insisted, then belied her words by saying, "We make a great team, and despite everything, we're going to make a

ton of money on this film. Out partnership is beneficial both in and out of bed. So, I say why stop? Let's
give America what they want and get back together."

Behind her, Maddie's eyes went wide.

"And what about what I want?" he asked, his eyes
pinned on the woman behind Natasha.

Chapter Twenty-Three

Talk about awkward. Maddie watched Natasha turn around to see who had Axel's attention. Maddie had come back to talk to Axel because she regretted her outburst almost immediately. Axel had been enamored with her face and her dress—which was all surface level, a fantasy for one night. Axel loved the fantasy, the fun. And Maddie thought she could play along. But that wasn't the real her. She had started to read more in his kisses, though she knew she shouldn't.

Like an addict, she hungered for more and feared what Axel gave her would never be enough.

It was time for this game to conclude. No sense playing something she would never win. If Natasha hadn't been able to settle him, who could?

Maddie had taken a minute or two to give herself

a pep talk before deciding to tell Axel she would end their fun.

But Natasha was all up in his space. Her white dress was embellished with crystals, and she wore her hair in big, oceanic waves that hung on her shoulders. She wore no jewelry and minimal makeup, and her skin shone under the light.

As soon as Natasha saw Maddie, her face twisted. "Hello, Maddie," she greeted her in a tone frigid enough to instantly cool boiling water. Maddie rubbed her arms, dubbing her the Ice Queen.

She forced her tongue to loosen. "Congratulations on your film premiere tonight, Natasha," Maddie said, being overly cheerful to appear unaffected under the Ice Queen's disapproving glare.

Natasha dismissed her by turning back to face Axel. "Think about what I said. I'm at the Ritz tonight, if you want to start on our reunion. I fly out to Colorado early tomorrow on a mission and could use a proper send-off."

After that, she was on her way. Maddie shook her head. Natasha was either bold, gutsy or clueless. Natasha had remained quiet while Axel endured major backlash on social media and now expected him to rekindle their relationship like it was nothing.

"I'm sorry you had to hear that," Axel said once they were alone.

Maddie strove to appear unbothered, but her chest felt tight. Jealousy had wrapped thick cords around her heart. "I'm not surprised." Peering up at Axel from under her lashes, she asked, "Are you going to consider her offer?"

"I've already dismissed it," Axel said. "I want to talk about your getting mad at me for paying you a compliment."

Her heart eased a little, but the jealousy wasn't letting go. To deflect, Maddie tapped the slim watch on her wrist. "Can we talk about that after the movie? We have to get to our seats."

He glanced at his watch and sighed. "All right, but we're having this conversation." He bent to whisper in her ear, "Then I'm going to kiss you senseless."

Maddie suppressed a shiver and followed his lead into the theater. Her mother, his parents and Lindsay were already seated in the front row of the center section. Most of the audience was also seated, talking in hushed tones, their murmurs creating a light buzz.

Before they parted ways, Maddie went into her purse to get a small bottle of Tic Tacs. She always made sure Axel had them. He slipped them into his pocket before strutting over to sit with his parents. Maddie went to sit next to her replacement a couple seats down on the left.

Two women approached and must have asked Axel for a photo, because he was back on his feet, his arms slung around both their waists and his smile wide. The women were gorgeous, their faces flawless. Standing together, all three were perfection.

Maddie shrank in her seat. She wasn't the type to wear makeup, to be a living doll on display. She was more of a lip gloss–and–mascara girl. It had taken

Faran close to an hour to work on Maddie's face. An *hour*. Maddie admired women who had the patience to bring their A game like that every day. But that wasn't for her, and she was all right with it. More than all right.

To her right was Donny Boothe, one of the actors with a minor role in the film. He nudged her. She gave him a smile and hoped he wouldn't see it as an invitation.

Donny's eyes homed in on her plunging neckline before he winked at her in appreciation. "What are you doing later?" he asked. "We can hang out at the afterparty." His breath was hot—like he needed a Tic Tac.

She wrinkled her nose. "I have plans." Donny had been a flirt on the set. He was one of those men who knew how handsome he was and acted like it.

"Well, if you change your mind..." He trailed off and waggled his eyebrows, searching in his pocket for a business card. He tucked it in her hand. Those were handy at these kinds of events. Deals were made and lost on the red carpet. Right along with relationships.

Maddie curled her fingers around the card, tempted to crumple it, but she didn't want to be rude. So, she slipped it in her purse. Feeling eyes on her, Maddie lifted her head. Her gaze collided with Axel's. He must have seen Donny hand her his card. She shrugged, as if to say, *What do you want me to do?*

Lindsay whispered in her ear, dragging Maddie's attention away from Axel's frown. "He gave me a card, too. I'll be filing this away in the trash can."

Maddie rolled her eyes. "You and me both. Can you imagine?"

Lindsay laughed and then took in Maddie's attire. "Hey, you and Axel are wearing the same shade of blue. Was that a coincidence or was it planned?" There was slight acid in her tone. Maddie wondered about it but decided to give an honest response.

"Axel suggested it," Maddie said, then wished she hadn't answered.

Lindsay pursed her lips and gave Maddie a calculating glance. Maddie could almost hear the questions in Lindsay's head. She shifted and clutched her purse. She was not about to answer to Lindsay.

Or feel like she had done anything wrong.

"I can't blame you, girl," Lindsay cupped her mouth and whispered in a conspiratorial tone. "Go for it."

Holding on to the plush theater seat, Maddie turned her head and arched a brow. "Go for what? What do you think is going on with me and Axel? Lindsay, do me a favor and stay in your lane," Maddie said, annoyed and not even trying to hide it. "Minding your own business will get you far in this job. This conversation is above your pay grade." Besides, she didn't know Lindsay like that. An impressive résumé had nothing to do with character. Or loose lips.

The other woman's face reddened. All she could do was nod.

Compassion flowed through her, and Maddie's irritation dissipated. She knew what it was like when you were just starting out and you needed to make yourself indispensable. Patting Lindsay's hand, Maddie strove to be gentler. "You were my top choice. Before me, Axel changed assistants quicker than he changed his underwear. I just want the best for you. So, I hope you take my advice."

Lindsay's head bobbed. "I have a lot to learn. I'm sorry for jumping to conclusions. I just thought you two make a cute couple."

"Well, regardless of how we look, we're not together." Maddie's heart pierced at those words. What she said was the truth. Axel was a professional at fun and games. And Maddie was his new toy. But what would happen when he found a newer, shinier one?

Yep. She would let Axel know their—what could she call it—momentary slip? Well, whatever. She was done.

And to prove it, Maddie gave Donny a tap on his arm and asked him for the address of the afterparty. He spouted off the name of the nightclub and she repeated it and gave him a thumbs-up sign, knowing she wouldn't go, but that had been a bold move for her. And she had spoken loud enough for Lindsay to overhear.

Artie Rae strode in and stopped to greet Faran. Maddie covered her mouth with her hand. She had forgotten about their appointment in her rush to get to Axel. This was another reason why she had to end things. She needed to focus on her career ahead.

Her mother kissed him on the cheek before she pointed in Maddie's direction. She threw Maddie a kiss and gave a little wave. Maddie waved back.

Artie beelined for her.

Her stomach tensed, and Maddie got out of her seat to meet him halfway. Artie was dressed in a bomber jacket, printed pants and black boots. He had long, dark hair with a nose ring. An earring shaped like a pointed cross dangled from one ear. Artie looked like a rocker, but he was a prodigy. His vision was sheer genius. At thirty-three, four of his films—and he had only done five—had been nominated for Oscars in several categories.

"You're quite lovely," he said in a British accent. "Just like your mum."

Maddie lowered her head briefly before she chided herself to accept his compliment. She met his gaze and smiled. "Thank you. I'm pretty excited for the chance to learn from you. I'm sorry I forgot to seek you out as we planned."

"Oh, I'm not bothered about that in the least," he said, then he rubbed his hands together. "I hope you're ready for it. I've been told I can be challenging to work with. Whatever that means," he said with a shrug.

"Bring it," Maddie shot back, liking that he could laugh at himself. Her stomach fluttered, thrilled to begin her new adventure.

He touched her cheek. "I'm sure we'll get on fine. Let's meet up tomorrow for lunch and work out the details of your internship." He walked to his seat with an unhurried stride and slipped between two leggy blondes.

Nico, the director, walked onstage, and the audience broke out in applause. Unlike Artie, he was clean cut and dressed in a black suit, white shirt and black tie. Unassuming until he spoke, Nico's attitude was that he preferred to add all the dazzle to his work. Those who were still standing scuttled to their seats. He lifted a hand, and the applause ceased.

"Good evening, everyone. Eighteen months ago, I had the pleasure of working with two of the most talented people in the industry. Axel and Natasha were a dream combination. Their talent is unequaled. I was fortunate to assemble an amazing team, and what we have created is something that we hope will take your entertainment experience to another level." He splayed his hands, and the curtains parted. "And now, get ready for the cinematic experience of your life. Ladies and gentlemen, I present to you, *The Mantis.*"

Chapter Twenty-Four

Axel used his fork to grab a piece of roasted cauliflower from Maddie's plate. After the premiere, Axel and Natasha had taken one more photo together before he and Maddie departed for the APL Restaurant located in the historic Taft Building. They sat in a cozy booth designed for two away from the entrance.

Their parents had decided to return to their suites and order takeout. He had them use the other SUV with his bodyguards. Call her a conspiracy theorist, but Maddie found their parents' retreat to the hotel suspicious. Convenient. It felt like…matchmaking.

She swatted at Axel's hand. "I knew you were going to do this. Why didn't you get your own?"

He popped the cauliflower in his mouth. "It tastes nicer coming off your plate."

"You have a serious case of food envy." She rolled her eyes and pointed to his rib eye with mashed potatoes and broccolini. "How's the steak?"

"Exquisite. Aged to perfection," Axel said, cutting a piece with his steak knife.

"It should be. You know that Adam Perry Lang makes his own steak knives? And he has a dry-aging room downstairs."

"Somebody's done her research," Axel teased.

"Always," Maddie said.

Growing serious, Axel said, "I'm going to miss you."

Unbidden tears sprung into her eyes. "I'll miss you, too."

"Now, do you care to tell me why you got angry when I complimented you earlier?" He leaned in and whispered, "And why you wouldn't let me kiss you once we were alone in the SUV? The windows are tinted."

She nodded and took a sip of her garden spritz, which had just the right of amount of rosemary. Then she licked her lips, pretending she didn't notice his hungry gaze following the path of her tongue.

"Axel, what you're seeing today is a mirage, a vision." She gestured toward her body. "This isn't the real me. I want to be seen, to be desired for who I really am."

He leaned close. "I kissed you when you weren't glammed up. So, this makes no sense."

"Yeah, well. You didn't see the look on your face. You looked...enamored, which, hearing myself say it aloud, I know is an exaggeration." She tossed her hair and shrugged. "I can't find the right word. But that look on your face scared me. Axel, you have thousands—no, make that millions—of women crushing on you, throwing themselves at you. I'm not one of them. I'm me."

"I like *you*," he said simply. "The you that speaks her mind. The you that is loyal and helpful. The you that's a great companion. That's the woman I know and like."

Maddie glared. "You just described man's best friend."

"I don't see you as a pet, but I do see you as a friend. There aren't many people in my life who I can trust, because I'm a celebrity. You're high up there on my list. Next to my family, it's you." He sighed. "I get the feeling that no matter what I say, you're going to have a problem with it." He tilted his head. "Let me ask you a question. If you don't want to be seen, to be noticed, then why did you go the extra mile, put in the extra time to get all fancy tonight?"

"I—I don't know."

"You do know." He pointed his index finger at her. "So, out with it, right here and now. What's the real problem?"

She opened her mouth, but he held up a hand.

"This friendship thing works both ways. I know you, and this isn't the issue."

Her throat felt tight, but Maddie forced the words out. She needed to be honest with herself—and her friend. "You're right. I wanted to get you all bug-eyed when you saw me. My getting fancy, to use your words, was all about you. But when you did…I got scared. Because I wanted to please you, but then I don't want to lose myself. And I feel I could. I could easily lose myself in you. And you're all about having a good time."

He nodded and gestured for her to continue.

She blinked back unexpected tears. "I'm not that person. I'm not spontaneous or carefree. I have a plan for my life. I have goals. I'm way too serious not to take anything we do together to heart. I'll want more. That's why I have to stop any physical interaction with you."

His eyes went wide. By his expression, Axel grasped what she was trying to say. He eased away from her a fraction, and Maddie's heart rebelled to her very core.

"I understand, and I agree. You deserve more. I'm attracted to you on a level that's hard to comprehend. But I can't offer anything more than this," he said.

She didn't want him to understand. She didn't want their kisses to end. She wanted him to consider giving them a chance. She wanted to see if the attraction between them could lead to more. She didn't want him to see her as he did the other women.

All her secret hopes and fears gushed out in one word. "Why?"

"That's the one thing—the only thing—I can't share with you, and I hope you'll respect me enough to leave it at that."

She wanted to protest, to push him for details. But Axel had closed off. His eyes darted around the restaurant, his body fidgeting. He undid the first button of his shirt and signaled to the server that he was ready for the check.

Maddie remained composed, but inside, her heart felt like it had been slashed by the claws of a large feline. She clamped her lips to keep from pleading with him to try. He rested his hand on her back as he escorted her out of the restaurant. Her traitorous body tingled, yearning for his touch. She shrugged him off, thanking him as he held open the door.

When they were in the SUV and on their way back to the hotel, Axel asked, "So, are you planning to take Donny up on his offer?"

She spun to look at him with disbelief. "No. Do I look desperate to you? I'm not interested in him."

"Good." He folded his arms, rested his head on the headrest and closed his eyes.

She pinched him. "Are you jealous?" she asked in a furious whisper, not wanting their driver to overhear the conversation. "You don't want me, but I shouldn't want anybody else?"

Rubbing his arm, he said, "It's not like that."

"Then tell me what it is like. Because you're confusing me."

He sighed. "Can you let this go?"

"Nope. Not doing it."

Once they were at the hotel, Maddie raced to keep up with Axel's long strides. He pushed the button for both their floors. But she refused to get out.

"Maddie, I need to get some rest."

"And you will. After you provide me with an explanation."

"Goodness, you're stubborn."

"Thank you for the compliment," she shot back.

Axel didn't say another word until they entered his penthouse suite. Maddie could feel the heat of his anger, his frustration, but too bad. The emotions swirling within her had the unpredictability of a tornado, and she was going with the flow. As soon as the door closed and they were alone, Axel snatched her into his arms and crushed his lips to hers.

Maddie only had one thought—she had voluntarily entered the panther's cave, and now she had become his prey.

Chapter Twenty-Five

From the moment he had seen her earlier that day, his body had craved to have her close. He had wanted to crush her in his arms. Once they entered his suite, he snapped, giving in to the urge. Axel expected her to push him away, but she didn't. Maddie curved into him, content, like she wanted to be in his arms.

After a few seconds, Axel tore his lips off hers and placed a kiss on her neck, loving the scent of her perfume. It was sweet and gave him a heady feeling.

"I saw you with him, and I didn't like it," he ground out.

Her brows furrowed. "Who?"

"Donny. I didn't like it." He tasted her soft brown skin. "What's that you're wearing?" he asked, tortured.

Maddie didn't answer, and he didn't mind. She

was like a well in the middle of the desert, quenching a thirst he didn't know he had. And boy, was he thirsty. The more he drank of her lips, the more he had to get one more taste.

"It's an essential oil called Lick Me All Over," she finally replied, holding his head with her hands, her breath sounding shaky.

Good. He wasn't the only one caught up with this sudden, overwhelming desire.

Axel groaned when her words registered. "Are you serious?"

"That's what it's called."

"Do you want me to?" he asked, trailing kisses back up to her neck.

"What?"

"Lick you all over."

"Of course. That's what I want."

Realization dawned, piercing his desire-filled mind. He knew Maddie's thought process. She wanted to prove to him that they could be in a relationship. That he could give her more.

He released her. "Is that why you insisted on coming to my suite?" he bit out, feeling trapped in the five-thousand-square-foot space.

"No, but I can't say I'm sorry about it," she said, her chest heaving.

Axel stormed away from her toward the huge windows, showcasing the beautiful night lights of the high-rise buildings in Los Angeles. The view should give him peace, but his mind was jumbled. He felt a pair of arms circle his waist from behind, and Maddie rested her head on his back.

For a few precious seconds, Axel placed his hands above hers and closed his eyes, treasuring the rightness of this moment. A rightness, a connection that made him want things he shouldn't.

Then she sighed.

A sigh overflowing with contentment. Like she was at peace.

He tensed, doubting his ability to maintain that state. His mother must have sighed that way many times, unaware of his father's unsettled nature. A wanderlust that made Kirk Smith deny the son who dared to find him. Deny Axel the chance to love him, to help him, to forgive him before he left the earth.

No. He couldn't hurt Maddie like that. She wouldn't find peace with him.

She sighed again.

This one sounded like she could stay like that forever. Panicked, he slipped out of her arms and turned to face her. "I have something to tell you," he said, hoping to offer her a tantalizing diversion.

Her lips looked flushed, kissed. "What is it?" She looked wary but expectant.

"Let me get comfortable first."

Maddie took that as her cue to take off her shoes. Axel led her to the couch in the sunken living room area and took off his jacket before he answered her. "I had Ralph submit your script to some Netflix producers."

Her eyes grew round. She jabbed him in the chest.

"I can't believe you did that! Why did you do that?" Without giving him a chance to speak, she cupped her cheeks with her hands and demanded, "Well, don't keep me in suspense. What did they say?"

"They want to buy the movie rights."

"I can't believe this," she whispered. "Netflix wants my script." Then she screamed, catapulting herself into his arms and causing him to fall backward on the couch. Maddie plastered kisses all over his face. "Thank you. Thank you. Thank you. I can't wait to see you as Brock."

Holding her steady, Axel sat up. He held her hands. "Yeah, Maddie. About that."

She tilted her head. "Uh-oh. What is it? Tell me."

"They don't feel I'm the right person for the film. They want to go with another actor."

"No," she said with vehemence. "I don't want anybody else but you. Have Ralph talk to them."

"Maddie. It doesn't matter," he said, giving her hands a light squeeze, though he was crushed. "This is about you and your project reaching millions. Your career is going to skyrocket, and I'm going to be rooting for you. When it comes to business, it's okay to be selfish. You have to help yourself before you can help others." He scooted close. "Just think of all the little Black girls you're going to inspire." Patting her hand, he said, "There will be other movies."

She mulled over his words and then nodded. "I'll give Ralph a call. I do feel bad, though, that Netflix didn't want to take a chance on you."

"They do," he said, glad for the segue. "Netflix

offered me the opportunity to star in *The Father She Needs*. It's a drama set in Colorado."

Her brows raised. "Oh, Axel. That's wonderful. When do you begin filming?"

"The sixteenth." He watched her facial expression change.

"That's three days before the school play."

"And your birthday," he supplied.

She smoothed out her dress. "So, what did you tell them?"

"I didn't. I signed the contract."

"Oh." Her shoulders curved. He could almost taste her disappointment. Tucking his finger under her chin, Axel lifted her head so he could look into her eyes.

"I'm sorry."

Using her hands to push herself to stand, Maddie said, "Excuse me. I'll be right back." Then she rushed into the bathroom.

When she returned, she was fresh-faced. Her cheeks looked flushed, and her eyes were red. She looked beautiful. He hugged her, using her stomach as his pillow. Axel couldn't take the silence.

"What are you thinking?"

"That you're selfish and I shouldn't have been surprised," she said, even as she cradled him. Her harsh words contrasted with her gentleness cut him to the core.

"It wasn't easy. And thinking of myself isn't being selfish. I call it self-care."

She pulled away, fire in her eyes. "Whatever helps

you sleep at night. The children are working their butts off because they think you're going to be there. Today is my last day. Day fourteen. But do you need me to show up on Monday to tell the students?"

"No. You don't have to tell them. Focus on packing. I need to do that myself." He stood and clasped his hands behind his back. "There is another option."

She folded her arms, which made her breasts swell under her gown. "I'm listening."

"I could be the executive producer and seek investors to fund your movie."

Chewing on her bottom lip, she said, "That's a big risk."

"I think the project is worth it. But Netflix is ready, and they have the money. All you have to do is sign on the dotted line." He then asked, "Do you think your mother would want to invest?"

She gave a little nod. "She would, but I can't ask her to do that. She has more than enough to live two lifetimes, but we both know you need serious capital. Especially for the movie I envisioned. I don't want to sacrifice quality or, worse, underpay the crew and cast."

He dared to take her hand. "Maddie, I love how you think of others, but in this case, it's okay to think of your chance at advancement. If I were you, I'd take the Netflix deal."

"You've given me a lot to think about," she said, yawning. "I'd better head to my room." She went by the window to collect her shoes. Remaining barefooted, Maddie went to the door. "Goodbye, Axel."

Those two words caused a crescendo of panic on the inside. Maddie opened the door a crack, ready to slip out of the door—and his life for good.

"Wait," he yelled. Surging to his feet, Axel raced over to where she stood. He placed his palm on the door and closed it.

"Don't go," he said, pleading, sandwiching her between his body and the door. "I'm the most self-ish man in the world for asking, but I will anyway. Maddie, stay. Stay with me tonight. Give me something to remember in the long nights ahead." His chest heaved and his heart hammered in his chest. While he waited, he closed his eyes, unable to bear her possible rejection.

He heard her shoes fall to the floor with a thud.

He saw her hand reach up to slip the dress off her shoulders.

He felt the whoosh of her dress as it fell to the floor.

Then he scooped her in his arms. It took hours for Axel to demonstrate how much she meant to him, how much he was going to miss her. She accepted all he had to offer, giving as good as she got. Replete, they fell asleep in each other's arms.

But when Axel opened his eyes the next morning, his hand rested on cool sheets. Maddie was gone.

Chapter Twenty-Six

"Maddie, are you here?" he called out.

Though it was futile, Axel darted through the other rooms in his suite, hoping to see her mop of hair peeking out from under the covers. But all remained untouched. His heart shattered as if it had been struck by a boulder.

He trudged into the shower, telling himself he had made the right decision, and forced himself to get dressed. His flight wasn't until later that afternoon, so he had most of the day to think about what he had let go. Maybe he would work on some of his cartoons to pass the time. If he could concentrate.

His mind was full of Maddie. Maddie's face during the height of ecstasy. Maddie's moans when he'd loved on her in all her secret places. Maddie. Maddie. Maddie.

Axel had just decided to order oatmeal for breakfast when his doorbell rang. His stomach felt full from sadness, but he knew he needed to eat.

Because he knew the penthouse could only be accessed by those with a special card, Axel wasn't concerned when he went to answer the door. It was the hired bodyguards. He greeted the men, who had come to check on him. He hadn't realized Maddie had kept them for the weekend. The burly men settled into two armchairs in the hallway, declining his offer of breakfast.

He had just closed the door when seconds later, the doorbell rang again. That must be his oatmeal. He grabbed his wallet and opened the door.

When he saw Natasha, his smile dropped.

"What are you doing here?" He didn't even try to be courteous.

"I'm here to discuss our travel plans," she said, stepping past him. She was in full makeup, dressed in a pair of designer sweats and her hair was in a ponytail. Looking at her, Axel wondered what he had ever seen in her.

"What do you want?" he asked, shutting the door for privacy.

"I told you. I need us back together." She stuffed her hands in her jacket pockets. Her smile was sweet, but her eyes were cold, calculating.

"You must be out of your mind," he shot back.

"Let's try to be civil since we're doing a movie together," she tsked.

"We *did* a movie. Past tense."

"Oh, didn't you hear? I'm playing your wife in *The Father She Needs*," Natasha said. "I signed on last night. Netflix is so pleased. They might even expand my role."

His lips curled. "I don't want to work with you."

"Well, you're going to have to. We might suck at a real relationship, but our onscreen chemistry is undeniable. Have you read the reviews for *The Mantis*? Our fans are begging for us to get back together. We need to market it. Together, we're bankable cash."

"After what happened on Drew's show, you really think they won't see our reunion as a publicity stunt?"

"My fans will believe what I tell them. My story is that you've apologized. Seen the error of your ways and because of my sweet, forgiving nature, I've given you a second chance." Natasha pulled out a small box and opened it. A diamond solitaire twinkled. "I plan to wear this when we debut our reconnection in public."

Cunning.

She had thought of everything.

Frustrated, he asked, "Why are you doing this?"

"Because you're not going to humiliate me by downgrading to your assistant. I won't become the butt of the jokes because you chose her over me." Her voice held bitterness. "I offered you a night in my arms, and you shunned me. For her."

"Humiliate you? You want to talk about humiliation?" he roared. "You did nothing. *Said* nothing while my reputation was ripped apart."

"A small price to pay for breaking my heart." Her voice caught. "I poured my heart out to you, and you turned me down. When I went home, I was devastated. So, no, I didn't care at that time that you were being dragged. But the next morning, I was going to post a statement in your defense when my agent called. *The New Yorker* wanted to feature me. Then more calls... I've done a perfume ad, a sneaker shoot and I'm even being considered for a clothing line. My net worth is going to double."

"All those endorsements are superficial."

"Tell that to my bank account," she scoffed. "My agent said if we got back together, there could be more possibilities. Greater opportunities."

"Wow. So, this isn't about any genuine feelings, it's about your pride. And money." Axel's nostrils flared. "And where did you get the idea that I chose anyone over you? I am a man of integrity. I was up front with you that I wasn't going to get married. And you know I don't sleep around when I'm dating. I won't be like my—" He stopped, not finishing his sentence.

"Yes, I know that," she interrupted, flailing her hands. "I'm not questioning your faithfulness."

"So why do this?" He shook his head. "I don't understand."

"Like I said, I have a reputation to uphold. All I'm asking for is three months. Three months and then you allow me to give you the boot." She held out a hand, expecting a handshake.

"I'm seriously questioning your sanity right now," Axel said, ignoring her hand. He found the idea of touching her repulsive. "Give me one good reason why I would go along with your harebrained scheme."

"I'll give you two," she quipped, pulling out her cell phone.

Axel's eyes went wide. She had pictures of Maddie. The first picture showed Maddie and Axel entering his suite together. The second showed Maddie leaving. There was no denying from her wild hair and crushed dress what she had been up to.

"What are you—a stalker now?" he hurled.

Natasha looked ready to slap him before she composed herself. "I don't stalk men. Men stalk me. Both times I captured her, it was mere coincidence. Last night, I was coming to seduce you, but you had other plans. This morning, I was coming to break the news of the movie when I saw her exiting your suite, obviously satiated. I was going to send you the pictures to taunt you, but then, I considered my agent's suggestion. I knew these photographs weren't coincidences, but opportunities."

Natasha helped herself to some water. "I have nothing against Maddie. She didn't do anything to me. But the reality is she means nothing. At least not to me. I have no problem posting these pics on social media and blaming her for our breakup."

Axel could tell from the set of her jaw that Natasha meant her threat. Her image meant more than damaging an innocent woman. How could he have dated someone so shallow for so long? Unless they were the same.

No. This experience had changed him. He had a ways to go, but he wasn't the same man. This experience had also changed Natasha, but not for the better.

He thought about Maddie's internship. Her movie. Her career. With a few strokes, Natasha could destroy that. Or set her back. Maddie wouldn't be able to handle that kind of backlash. She was too good and too kind.

"You're better than this," he pleaded, hoping Natasha would bend.

But she lifted her chin. "Three months."

Clamping his jaw shut, Axel gave a terse nod. "Fine." He would have to send Maddie a text to warn her, so she wasn't blindsided when pictures of them popped up on the internet.

"Great. I'm glad that's settled. We'll have lunch together and then we'll fly out to Colorado together."

The oatmeal arrived, and Natasha made sure the server saw them together. The young man's eyes widened. Axel groaned. There was no way he wasn't going to spread the news that Natasha LaRue was in Axel's suite.

He rubbed his temples, no longer hungry. Natasha dug into his oatmeal. Axel stood, watching her eat with relish, like she hadn't just threatened to destroy another woman.

She snapped her fingers. "By the way, this arrangement is between us. So don't even think about telling Maddie. Cut those ties and keep those sweet lips of yours sealed."

No. Rocks lined his stomach. He and Maddie had already parted ways, but it had been amicable. Axel had envisioned they would text to check on each other. Nothing serious. They'd keep it lighthearted. But Natasha didn't even want him speaking to her.

If he didn't warn her about going public with Natasha, Maddie would be crushed. She would think he had left her arms and returned to Natasha's.

"That's cruel," he breathed out.

"Those are my terms," she said, her voice hard, her tone defiant. "Give me your word."

"Fine," he ground out. His fingers curled. Axel wanted to scream, to punch a wall, but he knew Natasha wouldn't relent. She wore her stubbornness like armor. "I have to be back in Florida on Monday, so I'll meet up with you in Colorado."

"Fine." She shrugged. "I'll come with you. I can't have us going on separate flights right after I announce our getting back together. That would look too contrived."

Feeling claustrophobic, Axel exhaled. He whispered, "Natasha, I don't know if I can do this." She was all up in his world, in his space. It was overwhelming. Stifling. Axel couldn't help being grateful that he hadn't accepted her proposal.

"You can and you will," she said. "You're a phenomenal actor. Put those skills to good use."

He folded his arms. "I'm not sleeping with you."

She snorted. "Oh, please. Don't flatter yourself.

My proposition last night was a lapse in judgment. A case of hormones. I won't miss being in your bed, trust me. I want an Oscar. That's my goal. My prize. Oscar is the only man I want in my hands."

Chapter Twenty-Seven

Before this morning, Maddie had never done the walk of shame. Never understood the expression. But she sure did get it now.

Early this morning, Maddie had donned her wrinkled gown, stuffed her underwear in her bag and entered the elevator barefooted, her shoes in her hand. Thankfully, she had descended to her floor without anyone else joining in the elevator car to witness her morning-after face.

She had made love to Axel all night, and it had surpassed her expectations, her imagination. Maddie's screams had been operatic. It was a good thing the walls were soundproof and the bed solid wood.

Axel had given her more than a night to remember. It had been a night, dawn and daybreak to remember.

But once he had fallen asleep, her thoughts kept her awake. She'd pondered every word Axel had spoken and concluded that he really wasn't going to offer her more. He hadn't lied to her about that.

And for Maddie, that wasn't good enough.

As glorious as it had been between the sheets, that sensation was fleeting. She needed something more substantial. A life partner. And though she knew deep down that Axel could be the man who completed her, he had to know it, too.

That kind of confidence had to come from within. Axel had more growing to do.

So, she had to let any hope of a relationship with him go.

Thus, her walk of shame.

Jumping in the shower, Maddie allowed herself a good cry. A really, really long, really, really ugly, good cry. Because when she was done showering, she was done crying, she promised herself. Then she washed. Washed her hair. Twice. Washed the scent of him from her body, if not her mind. When she came out the bathroom, her skin was wrinkly and her lips chattered from the coolness of the room.

She cocooned herself under the covers and slept. She didn't awaken until close to noon.

Remembering her lunch date with Artie, Maddie jumped to her feet. She grabbed her cell and saw her mother had called. And texted. And called.

While she dressed, she called Faran. "I'm on my way to see Artie," she said. She started brushing her teeth.

"Okay, we can get together after if you'd like. Although Patrick and Tanya wanted to go see a play."

"Mom, we're going to spend months together on the movie. Go out with Patrick and Tanya. I've got plenty to do."

"Are you sure?" Her mother sounded hesitant.

"I am. Go hang with the Harringtons."

"How is Axel?" she asked.

Maddie coughed. "He was good the last time I saw him." Real good. Snoring-loud-enough-to-wake-a-sleeping-bear good. She gave herself a mental pat on the back.

"Oh, okay…" Faran trailed off, sounding let down.

"Talk soon, Mom."

Maddie's lips quirked. She wasn't about to tell her mother about her night in Axel's bed. That was privileged information. She might spill a little bit to Keri, but otherwise, Maddie intended to keep that night to herself.

She dressed in a pair of dress slacks and picked out bright striped shoes that coordinated with her top—how lucky was that—and went to the restaurant to meet Artie. She was the first to arrive, so she perused the menu before accepting a glass of water with lots of ice. While she waited, Maddie scrolled through social media reels.

She smiled at a clip of a dad and his triplets and the wife who had played a prank on her husband. She had just taken a slip of water when she came across a viral video with the caption Natasha and Axel at the Ritz.

Curious, she selected the clip and turned on the volume, hating her sudden, shaky hands.

A young man in sunglasses and a cap—his obvious attempt at a disguise—squealed into the camera, "Yo, get this. I'm on a break and you didn't hear from me, but I seen Natasha and Axel together in his suite. Seen it with my own eyes, yo. This is not a drill. Hashtag NatAxel is back in full effect, y'all. Ya heard it here first."

Maddie could hardly breathe. She gulped some of her water to keep from crying. Something she had vowed hours ago not to do anymore.

She played it again.

And again.

Until belief took root. It grew like a vine, wrapping itself around her heart every time she pressed Play. She couldn't believe Axel would sleep with her and then, hours later, go back to the woman who had created an internet scandal.

"Please tell me you didn't do that," she whispered, rubbing at her eyes. Maybe it was a stunt. She would call Axel for confirmation. Her phone slipped out of her sweaty palms and dropped onto the floor and under the table. Her arms weren't long enough, so she had to get on her knees and stretch to get it.

She bumped her head on the table. Great, her bun was going to come undone. Maddie heard a commotion behind her. Several people gasped. And she could hear excited murmurs, but she couldn't find out what was going on until she got her phone. Smoothing her hair, Maddie's hand curled around her phone.

She held on to the chair to stand. When she did, she saw Natasha and Axel. They sat two tables down from where she was seated and were the picture of love, arm in arm. Axel peered into Natasha's eyes, and even from her distance, she could see he was... besotted.

Sucker punched, she clutched her stomach and slumped into her chair. She gripped the edge of the table. Her cell pinged.

It was a text from Artie.

He was postponing their lunch appointment and sent his apologies. But Maddie was grateful for the reprieve. Now she had no reason to stay here, wading in this sea of mortification, her night with Axel now a torment. She sent Faran a quick text to say she was coming over, snatched her purse off the back of the chair and thrust it on her shoulder before storming out. Maddie didn't look back to see if Axel had spotted her. She kept her gaze firmly ahead.

As she was going through the exit, Tanya and Patrick were entering. He had invited his parents? That meant this reunion wasn't a stunt. Anger ignited. She felt used. And stupid.

Maddie would have kept walking, but Tanya called out.

"Maddie! I thought you were with Axel..." Her eyes narrowed.

It took every ounce of willpower for her to put a smile on her face. "No, I'm not with Axel." She wasn't about to mention whom he was with. She figured Tanya would find out soon enough.

Chapter Twenty-Eight

If she hadn't waved the picture, Axel would have abandoned their plan and raced after Maddie. His chest hurt, and he was already missing Maddie something fierce.

As soon as Natasha and Axel had entered the restaurant and he saw his Maddie crouched on the floor, Axel had felt the pull to join her. To explain. But Natasha held up her phone in his line of vision, making sure he remained compliant.

Giving her a hard look, Axel then transformed his face and demeanor to that of a man glad to be given a second chance. He viewed the next ninety days as a job that had to be done. A role in the movie that was Natasha's world. While Axel buried his misery,

Natasha stood at his side, preening and posing, the picture of sweet innocence.

Axel had invited his parents to the farce of a lunch. He needed their presence so he didn't have to talk to Natasha, knowing the extent of her vanity and self-absorption.

Patrick and Tanya strolled into the restaurant holding hands. He hated deceiving them, but just seeing them lightened his heart. Natasha made a big production of hugging and kissing them with tears in her eyes. The worst part was seeing Natasha flaunt her "engagement" ring. She made sure to capture a picture of the ring on her hand next to her salad to post on social media. It was all too much. Axel had to excuse himself with the guise of using the restroom.

During his restroom reprieve, he posed with a couple fans and signed napkins before returning to his table. When he did, only Tanya and Patrick remained. His tension eased a bit. He knew his parents would have questions.

"Natasha had a call from her agent and had to run. She said she would catch up with you later," his father said.

Axel nodded and opened the small leather folder holding the tab. He placed his credit card inside.

His mother reached over and tapped his hand. "Care to tell us what this is about?"

"Natasha apologized, so we decided to take our relationship to another level," was all he could say. "It's mutually beneficial."

Patrick shook his head. "Son, I know I've said

many times that marriage is a partnership, but you need more. Wasn't there a reason you turned down her proposal in the first place?"

"Yes, but I—I reconsidered."

"Axel, Natasha is a beautiful young woman, but you don't look at her the way you do Maddie," his mother said. "I mean, I thought…" She trailed off, shaking her head. "Never mind."

"I'm not worthy of her," Axel said, speaking the complete truth for the first time. The server came by to pick up the folder.

"You are, son, and then some." Patrick spoke with such confidence that Axel was tempted to believe him. If only it was Patrick's DNA in his blood.

"So you settle?" Tanya said.

"I'm not settling. Ever." He never intended to settle. Not with Maddie. And certainly not with Natasha.

Patrick addressed his wife, "Leave it alone, Tanya. The point of being grown is that you get to make your own decisions."

"Yeah, but can he live with them?" she asked.

He could for ninety days. But Axel didn't tell them that. He had to protect Maddie. "Can we talk about something else?" Axel pleaded.

His mother's brows rose. "You're back in love with a brand-new fiancée and you want to talk about something else?" She pinned Patrick with a knowing look. "Something isn't right about this."

The young man returned with his credit card, and Axel took the time to thank him and add a generous tip to his receipt.

"I have to agree with your mother, son," Patrick said, shifting his body to face Axel. "You don't look happy. Can you tell us what is going on?"

Axel drew a deep breath and stood. "Let's get back to the hotel. Then I'll tell you."

Tanya gathered her personal items, and they departed. Once they stepped into his penthouse suite, Axel unloaded. He told Tanya and Patrick about Natasha's plan and that she had threatened to accuse Maddie of breaking them up. He didn't mention that Maddie had spent the night with him or that Natasha had pictures of Maddie leaving his suite.

Tanya wrapped her arms around herself, her eyes filled with shock. "I can't believe Natasha would do something so underhanded. She gives off this soft aura."

"Yes, but she's a master at deception," Axel said. "Obviously, she had me fooled. But now my eyes are wide-open."

"You dodged a bullet there, son," his father said.

"I think we should tell Maddie the truth for you," Tanya chimed in. "If we explain, she would understand. You didn't see her face when we bumped into her at the restaurant. She looked crushed. Devastated."

"No. I gave my word," Axel said. He didn't want to think about Maddie's heartache. Telling her wouldn't change the fact that they wouldn't have a future. So, this situation might help her get angry enough to move on.

Patrick rested a hand on Axel's shoulder. "Wait

for an unguarded moment and try to record Natasha talking about this evil plan."

Axel chuckled. His father watched a lot of suspense shows, so he wasn't surprised he would suggest this. "That's a good idea, but I can't have Natasha retaliate in any way. She would find a way to spin things and make me the monster. After this whole scandal, I have no doubt I would end up being the bad guy."

"So, you're just going to wait out the ninety days," his mother said, her tone sympathetic.

"Yes."

"Keep her away from us," Tanya said. "I don't want that woman in our home. I can't promise to mind my mouth if she's on my turf."

He knew his mother meant it. "We'll be away on location for a good portion of that time, so I can definitely do that."

"Your secret is safe with us," Patrick said. "I'm glad for your success. Meeting Faran was fun and we enjoyed your premiere, but I can't wait to return home to our simpler life."

Axel found that he agreed with that feeling. "I'm sorry I won't be there for the students' performance. I bought them all this gear and equipment to soften the blow, but listening to Natasha go on today, all I wanted to shout was 'All those things you seek are superficial. They don't last. It's good to have nice things, but it's better to have genuine relationships.'"

Tanya had tears in her eyes. She touched his cheek. "Son, it warms my heart to hear you say that. There's nothing like family and good friends."

"I so agree. I don't know how you all tolerated me," Axel said. "The only person I thought about was myself. How can I benefit? How can I profit? I did whatever I wanted, throwing money and gifts at people, thinking that was good enough. Coming back home, I got to experience something authentic with those students. Watching the joy on the kids' faces, helping them build their acting skills, gave me a sense of accomplishment. And I did it because I wanted to—not at first, though. Maddie had to convince me, and I'm so glad she did. I didn't get paid. I didn't get press, but I feel like a rich man."

Tanya dabbed at her cheeks. "I'm so proud of you."

"Yeah, well, I had great examples. And Maddie rubbed off on me. She worked with those students when I wouldn't. When I saw how the students loved her, even though I was the celebrity, I decided I had to help them. But really, they were the ones who helped me."

Patrick hugged him. "If you had won an Academy Award or earned a star on Hollywood Boulevard, I don't think I would be as proud of you as I am now. I am proud to call you son."

Axel tightened his embrace, loving the feel of his mother's hand on his back.

Then his father asked, "I get that this film is a great career move for you, but if you feel this way about the children, did you make the right choice?"

That question stayed with Axel all the way back to Love Creek. All the way through the weekend. And when he delivered the news on Monday and saw the students surround him, wishing him the best, Axel marveled at their generosity and sacrifice. None of the students expressed sadness; instead, they all were happy for him, urging him to go. Even though he had disappointed them. And all he could give them were more empty promises and more gifts.

Of course, the students were thrilled to have Natasha in their midst. She soaked up their admiration and even left Lynx a financial donation to the drama club.

Lindsay and Natasha hit it off. So much so that Natasha threatened to poach his assistant. Axel handed her over. Lindsay would feed Natasha's ego and fawn over her.

He would find another.

"That went well. I'm glad I came, though I wish you had allowed the press to capture all that we did," Natasha said, settling into her private plane. "Those kids were grateful for all you did. You should feel good about yourself."

But he didn't. He felt shallow.

And he missed Maddie.

Chapter Twenty-Nine

For the opening night of the play, Maddie arrived dressed in a sensible pair of black pumps, dress slacks and a cream blouse tucked into her pants. She had straightened her hair and ditched her glasses for contacts. Faran had showed her how to apply her makeup in a way that she still looked like herself, and Maddie was becoming adept at it.

She had hired movers to pack her essentials for Oregon and had surprised her mother when she donated her entire shoe collection, trading them in for regular shoes. Faran had urged her not to, but Maddie was ready for something new.

Her mother had already left for Oregon, and after the performance, Maddie would head to the airport.

Keri would return to pick up Maddie's car.

She made her way to the front row and sat. The auditorium was packed, and she was grateful that the students had reserved a seat for her. Two empty seats, actually. Only Axel wouldn't be there. She noticed the students had placed a picture of him on the seat, and her heart constricted. Maddie snapped a photo. She hadn't spoken to him since the week before, and she doubted she would again for some time. But what the students had done was thoughtful, and she needed to capture that moment.

Opening the program, Maddie's heart expanded as she read through the cast bios. She had gotten to know the students and found herself wishing for each of them to do well. Lizzie came racing down the aisle to give her a hug. Jeff was right behind her.

They were already in costume, and the set looked amazing.

"We're so glad you came," Lizzie said with a wide smile.

"Are you kidding? I wouldn't have missed this for anything," Maddie said, touching Lizzie's chin.

Something was different. She squinted, taking in Lizzie's hair and her shoes. Then it registered. Her mouth dropped. "Oh my goodness, Lizzie. Your braces are off."

"Yes, I got them removed a couple days ago. Finally." The young girl beamed.

"How's your voice?"

"I'm good," Lizzie said. "Don't worry, Ms. Maddie. I've got this."

An announcement was made for all the cast to report backstage. Jeff and Lizzie waved goodbye and then took off. A few minutes passed, and then Mrs. Millner, the drama teacher, came onstage. She must have returned from her leave in time for the play. The entire room broke into applause, and everyone cheered.

"During my absence, I was worried about whether the show would go on," Mrs. Millner said. "But I heard my students had the best substitute teachers ever."

Another round of applause broke out, accompanied by some whistles.

Holding up a hand, Mrs. Millner proceeded to thank Axel and Maddie. They used the new lighting system to zoom in on her. Maddie shifted uncomfortably under the spotlight and was relieved when Mrs. Millner stated that the show would begin.

They dimmed the lights, and Maddie settled deep into the chair. The first scene began, and Maddie was so proud, she couldn't stem the tears. All throughout the play, Maddie remained glued, entranced by their flawless performance. She was searching in her bag for some tissues when someone sat in Axel's seat. Then a hand reached over to hand her one. She knew that hand. She knew that scent.

Axel.

He was there.

"Thank you," she said, keeping her eyes straight ahead. Her heart pounded in her chest like a bass drum. "I didn't know you'd be here," she whispered.

"I had to. I convinced the director to let me do

my scenes early this morning, and then I hopped on Natasha's plane to get here."

Her stomach caved hearing him mention Natasha's name with such ease. His fiancée. The one who'd gotten him to settle down when he said he wouldn't. When he said he was only interested in casual relationships.

She dabbed at her eyes and focused on the play, refusing to get sidetracked by her emotions. If Axel didn't think she was worth more than a few turns on a king-size bed, then it was his loss. She wouldn't swim in regret.

When the scene came where Maria and the Captain declared their love, Maddie touched her chest. Jeff gave an incredible performance. Axel reached over to take her hand. She peered over at him. He appeared to be caught up in the scene. She would bet he hadn't realized he had joined his hand with hers. Maddie curled her hand around his and held. The familiar tingle shot through her where they connected.

Then she remembered he had a fiancée waiting for him in Colorado and yanked her hand away. Folding her arms, Maddie tuned him out for the rest of the play until the curtains closed.

Then the cast came onstage to take their final bows, and the lights came on.

When the students spotted Axel, they squealed and darted off the stage to escort Axel to the front. He praised the students for their effort before a number of students walked in, holding bouquets for each of the girls.

Then Axel took the microphone and declared that he had established a scholarship fund for each of the cast members at the drama and theater arts program at Florida State University. Their eyes widened, and almost all the students broke into tears. Maddie was overcome at his generosity.

She looked toward the back of the room, expecting to see cameras, thinking Axel had done this for publicity and to rebuild his image. But there was no one. Axel hadn't done this for any other reason than to celebrate the children. To give them a chance at a future in the arts without the burden of hefty student loans.

That's when her heart cracked open. She admitted the truth. She loved this man. Loved him with an intensity that was exponential. Loved him so much that it scared her, because even now, if he said the word, she would forgive him anything.

Even for loving her with a passion the night before and then promising to love someone else the next day.

Yes, even for that.

That knowledge terrified her. Axel beckoned to her from the stage, mouthing for her to wait for him. But Maddie couldn't wait for someone who could never truly belong to her. She dashed out of the auditorium intending to jump into her vehicle before the crowd entered the parking lot. A large SUV was parked in front of the building, which Maddie assumed was waiting for Axel's departure.

As she drew close to her car, she frowned. There was a wrapped rectangular box on the hood. Maddie approached cautiously and held it up in the moonlight. She could see her name written in caps with a permanent marker in Axel's familiar scrawl.

Axel had remembered today was her birthday.

He must have gotten her a gift. And it wasn't in a Tiffany box, so she knew it wasn't earrings.

Curious, she tore open the wrapper and lifted the box. Inside was the most beautiful, unusual pair of shoes she had ever seen. They were gorgeous. They were exquisite. They were so her.

If she hadn't acknowledged she had fallen for him before, she would have now.

But, sadly, she couldn't keep them.

They were a gift from a man betrothed to another. Maddie didn't get down like that. So, she placed the shoes in the box, walked to the SUV and handed them to Axel's driver. "Tell him I said thanks, but no, thanks." Then she went on her way.

Chapter Thirty

He had one more month. One more month and then he would be done with Natasha for good. Sitting across his bed in the two-bedroom trailer he shared with Natasha, Axel rested on his pillow and dreamed of that day.

For the past sixty days, Axel had made himself the man Natasha wanted, and he had hated every second of it.

Oh, he was all right during the day. Acting was what he loved. Filming *The Father She Needs* had stretched him, and he had already had Ralph scouring for new roles. Axel would never admit it to her, but Natasha had been magnificent as his onscreen wife. He wouldn't be surprised if she got that Oscar she craved.

They did have a good professional partnership.

But it was the nights when he and Natasha were locked inside their private trailer that was most challenging. Though a decent size, it wasn't big enough for two forceful personalities. Each had acknowledged they couldn't stand each other. And they only addressed each other when necessary.

Yet she continued to present them to the world as a loving couple.

At night, Axel thought about Maddie. He missed his friend. He had gone from talking to her daily to nothing. Quiet. It was maddening.

Watching him suffer seemed to be Natasha's favorite pleasure. She liked knowing he was miserable. But Axel suspected she was jealous, and that prevented her from reneging on their agreement.

Natasha had caught him looking at Maddie's picture one night and taunted him, calling him lovesick. He had ignored her. For one thing, it was normal to miss someone you considered a friend. And for another, lovesick would imply that he was in love. Which he most certainly was not.

What he was, was tired of looking into Natasha's face at night. She was as annoying as a fruit fly, except he couldn't use a swatter on her. Axel had moved from sleeping on the love seat to the other bedroom.

Despite how he felt, Axel had kept his word. He hadn't contacted Maddie after the play, though he cyberstalked her on social media. He had purchased an iPad Mini just so he could have a portable stalking device. She had begun posting pictures of herself and her mother on set. When she posted a picture of her sitting in the assistant director's chair, Axel had been so proud.

She now wore her hair straight and dressed in variations of black and white. Her outward style had changed, but Axel didn't care. As long as she remained the same on the inside. That was what mattered most to him.

When he wasn't on one of Maddie's pages or working on his cartoon designs, Axel found himself on Love Creek High's drama club page. He checked in with the students often, Jeff in particular. Jeff was the only child of a single mom, and he worked after school to help her pay their bills. Axel had offered financial assistance, but Jeff had refused. Instead, he wanted to drop out of high school and move to Los Angeles to pursue his acting career.

As soon as he could, Axel intended to have a face-to-face with him and convince him to wait the few months and earn his high school diploma.

Natasha came by his room, standing at the threshold. She never entered his space, and he had never invited her inside. It was about fifty-three degrees, close to twenty degrees cooler than when they had started filming. Axel was ready to return to the Sunshine State.

Dressed in checkered pajama bottoms with a matching long-sleeved top that said Born to Act, and without the makeup, Natasha looked at least ten years younger. But Natasha had signed a contract with a cosmetics company, so her face stayed red-carpet ready in public.

"Have you thought about whether or not you're coming with me to celebrate my father's retirement on Wednesday night? I know the mid-week thing is weird but Daddy wants to retire on the very day he started his job thirty years ago." She had asked him a couple days before, on Saturday, but Axel had declined to answer, and the retirement party was in two days.

Axel looked up from his iPad Mini. He too wore flannel pajama bottoms, but he was shirtless. Something he would remedy due to her presence. He swung his feet off the bed and went to the large chest to get a T-shirt.

"No can do," he said, slipping his arm through the sleeve of his T-shirt. "I'm going to see my parents. Lynx and Shanna pushed up their wedding plans and have decided to get married this Saturday so I plan on going home this Thursday."

"That means I have to go," she groaned.

"You don't have to do anything. You're choosing to go."

"I'm supposed to be your fiancée. How does that look if I'm not there as your plus-one?"

"It would look like the truth," he said, his voice stern. "I don't want you to be my plus-anything. What I want is you out of my life."

"How about we fly out to my folks for the retirement party on Wednesday and then fly out the Thursday morning to Florida? I'm sure my family would understand me leaving early," she said.

His eyes narrowed. "Why do you want me there so bad? Is there something you aren't telling me?"

"My parents were upset that they had to hear about my engagement on television. They want to throw me—us—an engagement party at some point," she said. "And they can't be talked out of it."

"You had better try again, because an actual engagement party is taking this scam too far. Your father is very traditional, and I can see him coming for me because I didn't ask him for your hand in marriage."

She twisted her fingers together. "Yeah, he kind of said something about that."

"How did he feel about your proposal stunt?"

"He, ah, he wasn't too pleased with me. Felt like I should have waited for you to get on one knee." Her face reddened.

Axel could imagine Simon going on and on about that. He couldn't say he felt sorry for her, though. And he was firm about not going.

Picking up his tablet, Axel said, "I'm not getting ambushed by your father, and like I said, I have a previous engagement, so you'll have to figure something out. You're quite good at thinking on the spot."

Natasha smoothed her ponytail, though it had enough edge control and Jam that it wouldn't move in hurricane winds. "If you come, I'll cut our agreement short to end Thursday morning. Then in a week or two, I'll break the news to my parents that we decided to go our separate ways for good. My idea."

Her father must have been pressing her real bad for her to change their plans. Of course, Axel wanted to jump on the idea, but the imp inside him decided to take advantage of her desperation.

Feigning indifference, he said, "I'm good. I made it this far—what's thirty more days?" Besides, he knew her. Releasing him didn't mean she was going to delete the pictures. He needed Natasha to be very specific. That's how much he knew he couldn't trust her.

She squared her shoulders. "I'll delete the pictures. Completely. From everything."

"Prove it," Axel challenged. "Delete them now."

"I can't do that," she said, her eyes wide. "I'd lose my leverage. What's to keep you from backing out on me?"

He shook his head. This woman didn't know him at all. He couldn't wait to be rid of her. "My word, Natasha. You'll have my word."

Chapter Thirty-One

Faran held up a hand, her cheeks red. Puffs of cold air left her lips like tiny, dissipating clouds. She addressed the woman shivering before her. "I didn't raise you to be like this. Pining over a man who could never be good enough, even if he tried."

She delivered the words with enough venom that Maddie covered her mouth to stifle her gasp. Faran was exceptional.

"Cut," Artie yelled, sliding a glance her way. "Good work. Let's take five." He was tough with his critiques and stingy with his praise.

Everyone broke into motion. The makeup team went to freshen up Faran's face, and wardrobe brought out the winter coat Faran would wear in the next scene.

Maddie rubbed her cold nose and wrapped her coat around her.

It was forty-eight degrees in Portland. Forty-eight. Ten degrees less than the week before, and Maddie was feeling it. She spent most of her time in California or Florida, so her body wasn't used to these cold temperatures lasting all day. Yes, Florida got cold, but by the end of the day, the temperature would be in the high sixties. Not so here in Oregon. It would fall another ten degrees by sunset.

Pulling her knit cap over her ears, Maddie trudged over to where her mother stood and handed her a steaming mug of coffee. Faran was dressed in a white, faux-fur coat and a skintight white jumper befitting an ice princess traveling into modern times. They had been trying to get the scene right, but between flubbed lines and set mishaps, it had taken most of the day.

"Thank you, dear," she said. "My fingers are frozen stiff."

"We can start over with this scene tomorrow," Maddie said. "You don't have to keep running the lines."

"No, I'm ready to go home, and this is the last scene before we head to Florida and I can soak up that sunshine. It was nice of you to invite me as your plus-one to Lynx and Shanna's wedding."

"You're welcome, but I had selfish motives. I didn't expect to get an invite. But going to the wedding means I'll see Axel. And I need backup. I can't face him alone."

When Maddie left the restaurant after Axel flaunted his reunion with Natasha, she had headed straight to her mother's suite. Maddie had cried in her mother's arms for a long time, breaking her vow from that same morning not to break down again. Faran had held her and rocked her. When she was done, Faran had wiped her face and then ordered, "No more tears." Maddie hadn't cried since.

"Oh, honey." Faran rubbed her forearm. "You're exceptional, and it's his loss. There are many men out there if you decide to give them a chance."

Yes. There were other men who'd indicated interest. But she didn't want them. "They aren't Axel."

Her mother looked at her with sympathy. "You'll get over him soon. Soon he'll be a faded memory and a 'back then' story."

She doubted that. Maddie wanted Axel with a fierceness that clawed at her. At night, desire crawled up every inch of her body, igniting a burning, a fire deep within her core. Maddie ached for Axel to douse the flames, writhing and whispering his name. But every morning, she awakened, her passion unrequited.

Because he was engaged to another woman. A woman who wouldn't cultivate the best in him. Aside from her own pain, that was the hardest part for her to handle. All she could hope was that Axel would realize that himself and choose something better.

Something better—like her?

Yes, she admitted. Ugh. She needed to stop thinking about him. He had used her, rejected her and rushed back into the arms of his former love. Almost every time she went on social media, she saw their grinning faces, and her heart twisted.

But she refused to wade in the sea of self-pity. So, Maddie redirected her heartache into her work. Artie beckoned to Maddie, ending her conversation with her mother.

"Netflix called to ask me if I would direct your script. The casting director will be reaching out to Axel. Your gamble paid off."

"Finally," she said, her fists in the air.

"So, it looks like we'll be working together again real soon," Artie said. "You have serious potential." Artie had been demanding and stubborn, but the man was a genius.

"I'm looking forward to it almost as much as I'm looking forward to getting out of this cold," Maddie said, stuffing her hands into the pockets of her coat.

Axel cracked up before going back to review the film footage.

In a bold move, Maddie had declined to sign the contract with Netflix. Instead, she had asked Ralph to shop the script around, having signed on as his new client. But then the execs at Netflix decided to outbid the other offers, and Maddie had been shocked and exhilarated.

For the past sixty days, Maddie had taken the screenplay through the revision process. Before she hit Send on the final draft, Maddie had requested they reconsider Axel for the role. She had to applaud

Ralph. He had pushed for Axel to get the lead, and Netflix had agreed.

It was a win-win-win. A win for Maddie. A win for Netflix. And a win for Axel, if he accepted. Although the thought of seeing him and working with him for months gave her palpitations. Her mother said she must be hungry for punishment. Maybe. But also, she knew Brock couldn't be played by anyone other than Axel.

"Are you coming to the wrap party?" Artie asked.

Maddie shook her head. She didn't feel up to celebrating, and she had a good excuse. "My best friend is coming into town, and we have dinner plans."

He gave a nod. "You can always bring her if you change your mind."

Artie then signaled for shooting to commence, and Maddie returned to stand behind the camera. Artie had allowed her to direct the final scene. She was ready to showcase what he had taught her. She looked through the lens and made minor adjustments before calling out, "Action."

It took several takes before Artie gave a nod that they had gotten the shot.

The cast and crew burst into applause. They dismantled the set, everyone talking about the party. Faran headed back to her trailer to finish her last-minute packing. The wind started to pick up, causing leaves and debris to dance in the streets.

Maddie burrowed into her coat and braved the few blocks until she arrived at the restaurant. Keri had texted that she was already there and had ordered appetizers. Maddie spotted her as soon as she entered and rushed over to give her friend a big hug.

"What did you do to your hair?" Keri asked, looking at the top of Maddie's head.

Maddie touched her head. She had cut her hair into an edgy bob and then dyed the ends strawberry blond. Faran had freaked out when she saw it. "I needed a change."

"It's cute. I like the ombré effect." Keri pointed out. She wore a knitted sweater dress with thigh-high boots, and her brown camel coat was draped over one of the chairs.

They sat and perused the menu. Once they had placed their orders, the friends caught up on their lives. Keri had decided to get a roommate—with Maddie's blessing. Maybe she should sign her condo over to Keri. Her heart squeezed. She would, in time, but letting it go would be saying goodbye to her auntie again, forever.

"He's a college professor. Recently divorced. And he can cook."

"A man?"

"Yeah." She grinned. "Go figure. One big plus with a male roomie is that I don't have to worry about garbage duty. Remmie handles it."

Maddie arched a brow. Keri and her roommate had progressed to using nicknames? "Remmie?"

"Short for Remington." Keri couldn't quite meet her eyes.

Maddie's mouth dropped. "Oh my goodness. Don't tell me this is a roomie with benefits."

Keri shrugged. "I don't know. It just happened."

"His eggplant fell into your peach by accident?" Maddie cackled.

Keri snorted. "You are hilarious." Then she tilted her head. "Enough about me for now. How are you doing?"

The server brought their salads, so Maddie waited until he left to respond. Picking up her salad fork, she said, "My professional life is great. My personal life, not so much," before stuffing some leafy greens into her mouth.

"Have you heard from Axel?" Keri asked gently, taking a sip of water.

"Nope. Haven't seen him since the school play. He gave me an exquisite pair of shoes I'm pretty sure he ordered himself, but I didn't accept them. Didn't feel right taking a personal gift from an engaged man."

"I don't see anything wrong with a gift. He used to be your boss."

"Yeah. Used to. As in, not anymore."

"You're going to see him in a couple days. Are you ready for it?"

"As ready as I am to go to the North Pole," she joked. Just the thought of seeing Axel had her heart hammering in her chest. But to have to watch him smooching up to Natasha, that would be torture.

"Maybe you shouldn't go, then," Keri suggested.

Maddie lifted her chin. "I'm going, and my mother already postponed her flight to France to come with me. Besides, I'm not going to hide or run from Axel

Harrington and possibly feed his ego. My pride won't let me do that."

"Good for you," Keri said. "Have you found your dress yet?"

"Have I ever," Maddie said. "It's a cross between naughty and nice. Haute couture. I don't need a fairy godmother when I have a mother who's a super-model." She pulled out her phone and pulled up the photo app. Scrolling down, Maddie found the dress and showed it to Keri.

Keri rubbed her hands together. "I wish I could be there to see the look on his face when he sees you in that number. I can't even imagine you wearing a dress like that a few months ago. You've reinvented yourself."

"I would wear it even if he wasn't going to be there. And I wouldn't call it a reinvention. I would call it a discovery. I was all about loving myself, but at the same time, I was hiding under all this self-doubt and poor confidence and didn't know it. Now, I'm just about being me, whoever that is. And I'm having fun finding out, living in the moment, being spontaneous." She smiled. "I guess I have to thank Axel for that. He was all about having fun," she said with slight bitterness.

Their food arrived, and Maddie sniffed, appreciating the tantalizing smell. She had ordered a large, greasy burger and Keri the chicken sandwich. Everything came in jumbo portions. Maddie already knew she was going to need a couple of to-go boxes.

The server cleared their salad plates to make room for their meals on the small wooden table.

"Have you considered that just as you changed, he could have, as well?" Keri asked, cutting her sandwich in half.

"I don't think so. He's been on social media showering Natasha with gifts, flowers—you name it. That's a man who is very much about the superficial." Maddie worked the dull butter knife through the burger to split it in half, as well. She had to keep her hand firmly on top of the bun to keep the burger together. That's how large it was. But her first bite made her moan. It was juicy goodness wrapped in a soft blanket.

Keri pursed her lips. "You can't always believe social media posts, Maddie. People smile hiding their sorrow, their abuse. And you know I know about that."

Suddenly, her memory jarred. Her brows creased.

"What's going on?" Keri asked.

Wiping her mouth, Maddie placed her burger on the plate and racked her brain. "When I was leaving the restaurant that day, Tanya clutched my hand and said Axel had a message for me."

"What did he say?"

"He said to remember the saying about belief. I must have shoved it out of my mind. I was pretty upset that day. But just now, when you started talking about not believing what you see on social media posts, something clicked." Maddie leaned back into her chair. "I wonder why he said that."

Shaking her head, Keri said, "I'm not following you. What saying?"

"I once told Axel about my father's saying. I don't know if it's only a Jamaican saying or an actual proverb—"

"What is it?" Keri interrupted, gesturing with her hand for Maddie to get to the point.

"The saying goes, 'believe none of what you hear and half of what you see.'" She snapped her fingers. "Maybe he was trying to tell me something. Like I shouldn't believe what he said to me?"

Keri mumbled the words twice. Then her eyes widened. "He wasn't talking about you. It was a warning. I think he was trying to tell you about him and Natasha. Don't trust anything you're seeing and hearing about them on social media." She sat back and grinned. "Their relationship is all an act. A publicity stunt. I would bet my next paycheck on that."

Maddie shook her head. "If that's true, why wouldn't he tell me that? Why hide it from me?"

"That's something you'll have to ask him yourself when you see him."

Hope sprang, but fear made her question—made her wonder if this wasn't a case of wishful thinking. "What if you're wrong?"

Keri jabbed her thumb onto the wooden table. "The real question is, what if I'm right?"

Chapter Thirty-Two

Axel was free. He had endured the retirement evening with her folks and played his final scene as her fiancé. Now he was liberated from Natasha. This time for good and on somewhat amicable terms. Well, as amicable as one could be after being blackmailed for sixty days.

Natasha had deleted the pictures in an act of faith, and Axel had kept his word. He had smiled and doted on her, putting her parents at ease. Then, he had jumped on a plane the next day to get back to his life.

Today, as he stood in the hotel room, getting dressed for Lynx's wedding, anticipation bubbled within him at the thought of seeing Maddie. His Maddie. If it weren't for the fact that he had promised Lynx to be here a couple days early, Axel would have been in Portland, on bended knees, begging Maddie for a second chance.

However, he had consoled himself with the knowledge that he would see her today. He adjusted his tie and tapped his chest to ensure he had the rings.

Since they had invited a small number of guests to the hasty wedding, Lynx and Shanna had limited their wedding party to two bridesmaids and groomsmen. Lynx had chosen Axel and Hawk to stand with him, and Axel had been honored to perform the duty of holding the rings. Hawk had been in charge of the bachelor party—or rather, brunch—earlier that day. It consisted of the Harrington men catching a game and ordering pizza. Axel had invited Jeff to tag along. The teen had enjoyed himself immensely.

In lieu of gifts, Lynx and Shanna had requested donations to Alzheimer's and dementia patients as a token of love to Shanna's mother.

Rubbing his smooth face, Axel smiled to check his teeth, though he had brushed them before getting dressed. He scooped his wallet, hotel keys and Tic Tacs off the top of the chest and dropped them into his pants pocket. Looking at his watch, he saw that he was actually an hour early. Lynx had already warned him not to be on celebrity time.

Axel drove the short distance to his parents' house. Lynx and Shanna had transformed the backyard for the venue, since the place they had chosen had had a pipe burst. There was more than enough room to hold the outdoor wedding and host the reception. He skipped going through the front door, walking to the backyard.

He stopped, stunned at the transformation. Directly ahead was a seven-foot-tall wedding arch, with white and gold fabric drapes and hanging rose leaves. Gold Chiavari chairs lined each side of the aisle, and there were lights wrapped around the palm trees with hot air balloon paper lanterns. It was elegant and charming. The reception would take place under the large tent on the other side of the lawn.

The temperature was a balmy seventy degrees without a cloud in the sky, so he didn't anticipate any rain, but with Florida, you never knew. From where he stood, he could see large candles serving as centerpieces on the tables and knew by the waft of wind they were vanilla scented. He sniffed, appreciating the warm, pleasing scent.

Most of the guests had already arrived, helping themselves to appetizers, and the deejay was already playing some light jazz.

A bright light flashed before him, and Axel blinked with shock. The photographer thanked him and moved on. He noticed there were two additional photographers and a videographer to capture every moment. Axel marveled at their organization. He made a mental note to get that person's contact information. Not that he planned on getting married... Did he?

There was an attendant at the entrance to greet the guests and to provide the table seating. Axel went over and signed the guest registry. Then he persuaded the young woman to change Maddie's seat to next to his. Since Natasha wasn't coming, the spot next to him was available for Maddie.

The young woman then pointed to the sign that said all guests had to check their cell phones and electronics, which Axel could appreciate. He handed over his phone and accepted the small bracelet with his phone's ID number. Lynx and Shanna had ensured that Axel and Hawk could attend and maintain privacy.

Of course, Axel thought of Maddie. He could enjoy time with her without worrying that his face would end up on a tabloid magazine.

Axel scanned the crowd. If he knew Maddie, she was here already. He searched for her but didn't see her. Then he sighed. She might be inside.

Just then, Axel spotted a woman with lush curves, dressed in a figure-hugging purple dress, except her hair was cut short and straight. She was talking to his mother under the tent. He took a step. From behind, that looked like Maddie.

Then she turned and saw him.

And his breath caught.

And his heart skipped a beat.

And he had to remind himself to breathe.

Axel felt his eyes go wide. It was her. That was Maddie. He raked his eyes over her body as she took a tentative step in his direction. To Axel, she appeared to glide as she approached, and he remained transfixed, unblinking, hungry, feasting his eyes on the woman who had haunted his dreams.

"Fancy meeting you here," she said in a sultry voice.

"I was hoping I'd see you before the ceremony starts."

She raised a brow. "Why?"

He led her inside and into the bathroom.

As soon as the door closed, Axel rushed out, "I know we have plenty to talk about. Natasha and I aren't together. I know I owe you a proper explanation, but I just… I just need to…"

He snatched her close and pressed his lips to hers. Like a hungry man who hadn't eaten in days, Axel feasted on her sumptuous lips. Her shocked gasp filled his mouth, and he used that opportunity to plunge into the open space. Axel thought Maddie would push him away, but to his surprise, her small hands circled his waist. He edged closer and deepened the kiss.

Maddie's hands moved from his back up to his neck. Her little moans drove him into a sensual haze, into oblivion. The only thing that mattered was Maddie. He cupped her generous bottom and gave her a gentle squeeze. When she groaned, it incited him further. The small bathroom was a little confining, but all he could picture was bending Maddie over and… No. No. He couldn't take her like this.

Eventually, a loud sound penetrated his mind. Wait. Was that…knocking?

"Axel?" his father called out.

He tensed. Whoa! He had forgotten where he was. Lynx was probably looking for him. Maddie pushed out of his embrace. She appeared dazed—eyes full of questions. Axel covered her lips with his fingers.

"I'll be out in a minute, Dad."

"Hurry up. Your brother is looking for you."

"One minute, Dad."

She cupped her mouth and whispered, "Your father is going to know what we were doing in here."

"I've got it handled," Axel said, improvising. He dug into the medicine cabinet and pulled out some gauze. Then he wrapped Maddie's hand.

"He's not going to buy this," she whispered, giving him a shove.

Opening the door, he said, "That bandage should hold, but you need to get it checked out."

Seeing an empty space, he ushered Maddie out of the bathroom with her hiding behind him. Axel released a quick laugh, relieved. He turned the corner and almost ran into his father's chest.

Patrick gave him a knowing look and held on to his forearm. "Son, I need a word with you."

Maddie mumbled a quick, "I'll see you out there," and rushed past Axel and his father.

He called after her, "You just going to leave me like that? Oh, I see how you do."

She spun around to give him a shrug and wave before dipping outside. Axel traipsed after his father, who took him into his study. Once they were inside, Patrick rounded on him.

"Care to tell me what's going on with you and Maddie?" he asked, rubbing his beard.

"What do you mean?"

"Son, you have dated a myriad of women in the past, and I have never interfered. But those women were worldly, sophisticated. Maddie isn't like that. She's innocent. She's going to think it means more." He cocked his head. "Plus, as far as the world is concerned, you're engaged to Natasha. Do you want Maddie attacked because of your thoughtless actions?"

Axel stuffed his hands in his pockets. "I'm not being thoughtless. Believe me, I have done nothing over the last sixty days but think of her. And I wouldn't take advantage of Maddie in any way."

"Leave her alone, son," Patrick said, his expression fierce. "You have a thousand other women panting after you. I care about Maddie, and I don't want her getting hurt."

"I'm not trying to hurt Maddie," Axel yelled, frustration building. "And I can't believe you'd think I would do that."

"Not on purpose."

"Not ever."

"How do you know that?" Patrick shot back.

"Because I love her!" he shouted. "I love her. Love her to the point of madness. I know you think I'm all about fun, but trust me, falling in love is not fun. It's like I've fallen backward over this precipice and all I'm doing is falling and there is no stopping that from happening, no matter how hard I try." He grunted, wanting to howl and scream. His chest heaved. "I can't control it, and I have tried. So don't ask me to stay away from her, because I can't."

Patrick's mouth popped open, and then he smiled

slowly. "You are in love." He folded his arms. "So, what do you plan to do about it?"

Axel's left eye ticked. He blinked. His fury ebbed. "I...I don't know."

"She's not the girl you love and leave. She's the kind you marry."

"I want to," he choked out. "I want to marry her, but I have my father's DNA."

Patrick's brows furrowed. He placed a hand on Axel's back. "What does that have to do with anything?"

"My father left. Got on a Greyhound bus and left, and he never looked back. For no good reason. He not only abandoned Mom, he abandoned me. Wanted nothing to do with me." Tears threatened, but he refused to cry. "But as soon as I could, I found him. I went to see him, and when I did, do you think he apologized?"

"What happened, son?" Patrick asked, eyes filled with empathy.

"He...he rejected me." Axel fell to his knees, heedless of his expensive slacks. "He was dying and I offered to be a donor and he told me no. Even on his deathbed, my father thought I wasn't worthy. So, how can I be anybody's husband?" The tears trekked down his face. "I have his blood running through my veins. How can I be sure I won't do the same thing?"

Patrick bent over to look him in the face. "Because you're your mother's son. You also have her DNA, and she isn't a quitter. She is a fighter."

Axel lowered his head to his chest, his tears pouring out of pain, and renewal.

"I'm proud of you, son. You're not like my son. You *are* my son. I raised you. I taught you to be a better man. And you are. Better than thousands of men. You have honor. Integrity. And when I say I am proud of you, don't take those words lightly. I wouldn't say them if I weren't. You want to know how I see you? I see you as more than. More than a face. More than being famous. What you are is worthy. Worthy of love and being loved."

His father's words sank deep into his core, squeezing out any fear and doubt. Axel lifted his head and looked into his father's welcoming face. A face filled with love for him. For the man that he was.

Once their eyes met, Patrick commanded, "Get on your feet, son, and go get your woman," and held out his hand.

Axel puffed his chest, placed his hand in his father's and stood.

Patrick took out his handkerchief and wiped Axel's face. Axel felt like he was five years old again, but his heart expanded.

"The only time I want to see you on your knees like this again is if you're asking that lovely young woman to marry you," Patrick said. "Understood?"

Axel knew that tone. His father wouldn't accept any argument. "Understood."

Chapter Thirty-Three

Every movement she made, she felt the heat of Axel's eyes on her. Goodness, he was going to make it obvious that there was something going on between them. Even now, her lips sizzled with the remembrance of his kiss.

The wedding was both sentimental and beautiful. Maddie hadn't been able to hold back her tears through the ceremony. Shanna looked stunning in a vintage beaded ivory dress made of silk and lace. She had done her hair in soft curls, which made her appear ethereal. Everyone, including Maddie, had gasped when Shanna walked down the aisle, clutching a bouquet of exquisite lilies.

While Lynx and Shanna recited their vows, her eyes kept colliding with Axel's. He looked at her, mouthing the words. Maddie's heart raced, feeling like the spotlight was on her, like everyone had noticed.

But Axel didn't care.

It didn't help that she had been placed next to him for the reception. Axel was using every opportunity to make physical contact. His arm brushed hers when he picked up his utensils. His elbow grazed her breast when he reached for the Italian bread. Maddie suspected that was no accident.

The only time he left her side was to perform his duties as best man.

It was time for the cake cutting. Maddie felt a hand on her leg under the table, imprinting her flesh with his heat. Then he slipped his hand under the slit in her dress.

"Axel, behave. What are you doing?" she whispered, closing her legs tight. "My mother is here. Your parents are here. And Hawk is looking." His brother was seated across from them and had been tossing Axel hard looks, which Axel ignored.

"They can't see me," he said with an impish grin.

She bit the inside of her cheek. The man was a mess. "Still." She raked a hand through her bob, missing her curls. At least they would have covered her face.

"Are you ready to get out of here?" he whispered in her ear. His voice in her ear made her toes curl.

She was, but she wasn't about to tell him that. "I'm hungry, and I need to eat." Her mouth watered for the salmon, asparagus and potatoes she had ordered.

"I'm hungry, too—for something else. And eating is overrated."

"Speak for yourself." Maddie hadn't eaten since breakfast.

He clutched his chest. "Tossed to the side for food."

The good thing about their assigned table was that they had been served right after the bride and groom. Maddie dug into her meal, eyeing Axel's plate. He had chosen the chicken cacciatore. It smelled and looked delicious.

"Keep your eye on your own food," he teased, dipping his fork into his meal. He took a few bites and then leaned close. "Hurry and eat, because as soon as we're done, I intend to tell you I love you."

"What?" she squeaked out, twisting to look at him.

Axel went back to his plate with a calmness, like he hadn't just stopped her world.

Had he just said he loved her like he was talking about the weather?

Maddie dropped her fork on her plate, stood and dragged at Axel's arm until he got to his feet. She tugged him out of the tent and across the lawn and into the gazebo. It was fairly dark, so she was sure they wouldn't be spotted.

"What did you say to me just now?" she demanded, trying to make out his features in the moonlight.

"I do, Maddie," he said. "I love you, Madison Henry."

"But a New York minute ago, you got engaged to Natasha. The very next day. After you left my bed."

Thinking about that made her seethe. "What kind of game are you playing?"

"Natasha took pictures of you coming and going from my suite. She threatened to tell the world you were the reason I refused to marry her."

Maddie's eyes went wide. "Wow." So, Axel had been trying to protect her. "What did I ever do to her? And why didn't you tell me?"

He moved close and took her arm. "Do we have to do all this talking? In every romance scene I've ever done, we'd be kissing by now. After the hero declares his love, he dips the heroine and delivers a mind-searing kiss. That's how it's supposed to go. Yet, all I'm getting is questions and suspicions."

"Can you blame me?" she asked. "You insisted that you wanted to keep things light. So, what changed?"

"You. You changed me," Axel said. "I went from thinking of myself to thinking of you. Natasha noticed that I'm different when it comes to you. I was hollow, shallow, but when it came to you, I was... more. She couldn't handle that. You don't want to know how many times she begged me to fire you and I couldn't understand why." He lowered his voice and snaked his arms around her. "But I couldn't. I couldn't, because I valued you. I didn't recognize it as love at the time, but I just knew I couldn't let you go."

He led her over to the bench to sit.

Maddie's eyes brimmed. She swallowed. "Wow." That was all she had the breath to say.

"Yes. Wow." He hugged her close to him. "I've never experienced this before. This wow feeling."

Belief began to work through her heart and mind. She pulled away slightly and cupped his cheeks. "I love you, too, Axel. I know I can do really good by myself, but I'm better with you. You think I'm good for you, but believe me, you're good for me."

His eyes held wonder. "You mean that?"

"Yes. Of course I do." She wrinkled her nose. "Why do you find that hard to believe?"

"One day I'll tell you about my biological father. How he affected me." His voice held a vulnerability that she had never heard before.

Maddie kissed him tenderly and smiled. "This might seem strange, but when I look at you, I see Patrick. I forget he's not your biological father."

For seconds, Axel looked at her. "You really think that?" This time he sounded choked up.

When she nodded, Axel grabbed her into his chest and began to laugh. Kissing the top of her head, he said, "Oh, Maddie. I love you, and I have a feeling it's going to take a lifetime for me to tell you how much."

"A lifetime?"

"Hmm," was all he said, his eyes mysterious.

Maddie's heart thumped. Axel sounded like he was talking about an actual commitment. Like marriage. Axel stood and scooped her up in his arms so she had no choice but to straddle him.

She licked her lips, prepared to ask him about his lifetime comment. "What do you mean—"

He hemmed her in against the edge of the gazebo.

"No more questions," he said, "Give me my happy-ever-after ending." Then he kissed her. Kissed her and kissed her until Maddie had no more words to say.

Well, for that day, anyway.

* * * * *

*Don't miss out on the first book in the
Seven Brides for Seven Brothers miniseries,*

Rivals at Love Creek

*Available now from
Harlequin Special Edition!*

**WE HOPE YOU ENJOYED
THIS BOOK FROM**

HARLEQUIN
SPECIAL
EDITION

Believe in love. Overcome obstacles. Find happiness.

Relate to finding comfort and strength in the
support of loved ones and enjoy the journey
no matter what life throws your way.

6 NEW BOOKS AVAILABLE EVERY MONTH!

HSEHALO2020

COMING NEXT MONTH FROM

⊞ HARLEQUIN®
SPECIAL EDITION™

#2935 THE MAVERICK'S MARRIAGE PACT
Montana Mavericks: Brothers & Broncos • by Stella Bagwell
To win an inheritance, Maddox John needs to get married as quickly as possible. But can he find a woman to marry him for all the wrong reasons?

#2936 THE RIVALS OF CASPER ROAD
Garnet Run • by Roan Parrish
When heartbroken Bram Larkspur finds out the street he's just moved onto has a Halloween decorating contest, he thinks it's a great way to meet people. He isn't expecting to meet Zachary Glass, the buttoned-up architect across the street who resents having competition...and whom he's quickly falling for.

#2937 LONDON CALLING
The Friendship Chronicles • by Darby Baham
Robin Johnson has just moved to London after successfully campaigning for a promotion at her job and is in search of a new adventure and love. After several misfires, she finally meets a guy she is attracted to and feels safe with, but can she really give him a chance?

#2938 THE COWGIRL AND THE COUNTRY M.D.
Top Dog Dude Ranch • by Catherine Mann
Dr. Nolan Barnett just gained custody of his two orphaned grandchildren and takes them to the Top Dog Dude Ranch to bond, only to be distracted by the pretty stable manager. Eliza Hubbard just landed her dream job and must focus. However, they soon find the four of them together feels a lot like a family.

#2939 THE MARINE'S CHRISTMAS WISH
The Brands of Montana • by Joanna Sims
Marine captain Noah Brand is temporarily on leave to figure out if his missing ex-girlfriend's daughter is his—and he needs his best friend Shayna Wade's help. Will this Christmas open his eyes to the woman who's been there this whole time?

#2940 HER GOOD-LUCK CHARM
Lucky Stars • by Elizabeth Bevarly
Rory's amnesia makes her reluctant to get close to anyone, including sexy neighbor Felix. But when it becomes clear he's the key to her memory recovery, they have no choice but to stick very close together.

YOU CAN FIND MORE INFORMATION ON UPCOMING HARLEQUIN TITLES, FREE EXCERPTS AND MORE AT HARLEQUIN.COM.

HSECNM0822

SPECIAL EXCERPT FROM

H HARLEQUIN
SPECIAL EDITION

*When heartbroken Bram Larkspur finds out the street
he's just moved onto has a Halloween decorating
contest, he thinks it's a great way to meet people.
He isn't expecting to meet Zachary Glass, the
buttoned-up architect across the street who resents
having competition...and whom he's quickly falling for.*

Read on for a sneak peek at
The Rivals of Casper Road,
the latest in Roan Parrish's Garnet Run series!

He opened the mailbox absently and reached inside.
There should be an issue of *Global Architecture*. But the
moment the mailbox opened, something hit him in the
face. Shocked, he reeled backward. Had a bomb gone
off? Had the world finally ended?

He sputtered and opened his eyes. His mailbox,
the ground around it and presumably he himself were
covered in...glitter?

"What the...?"

"Game on," said a voice over his shoulder, and Zachary
turned to see Bram standing there, grinning.

"You— I— Did you—?"

"You started it," Bram said, nodding toward the
dragon. "But now it's on."

Zachary goggled. Bram had seen him. He'd seen him do something mean-spirited and awful, and had seen it in the context of a prank… He was either very generous or very deluded. And for some reason, Zachary found himself hoping it was the former.

"I'm very, very sorry about the paint. I honestly don't know what possessed me. That is, I wasn't actually possessed. I take responsibility for my actions. Just, I didn't actually think I was going to do it until I did, and then, uh, it was too late. Because I'd done it."

"Yeah, that's usually how that works," Bram agreed. But he still didn't seem angry. He seemed…impish.

"Are you…enjoying this?"

Bram just raised his eyebrows and winked. "Consider us even. For now." Then he took a magazine from his back pocket and handed it to Zachary. *Global Architecture.*

"Thanks."

Bram smiled mysteriously and said, "You never know what I might do next." Then he sauntered back across the street, leaving Zachary a mess of uncertainty and glitter.

Don't miss
The Rivals of Casper Road by Roan Parrish,
available October 2022 wherever
Harlequin Special Edition books and ebooks are sold.

Harlequin.com

Copyright © 2022 by Roan Parrish

HSEEXP0822

Get 4 FREE REWARDS!

We'll send you 2 FREE Books <u>plus</u> 2 FREE Mystery Gifts.

FREE Value Over **$20**

Both the **Harlequin® Special Edition** and **Harlequin® Heartwarming™** series feature compelling novels filled with stories of love and strength where the bonds of friendship, family and community unite.

YES! Please send me 2 FREE novels from the Harlequin Special Edition or Harlequin Heartwarming series and my 2 FREE gifts (gifts are worth about $10 retail). After receiving them, if I don't wish to receive any more books, I can return the shipping statement marked "cancel." If I don't cancel, I will receive 6 brand-new Harlequin Special Edition books every month and be billed just $5.24 each in the U.S. or $5.99 each in Canada, a savings of at least 13% off the cover price or 4 brand-new Harlequin Heartwarming Larger-Print books every month and be billed just $5.99 each in the U.S. or $6.49 each in Canada, a savings of at least 20% off the cover price. It's quite a bargain! Shipping and handling is just 50¢ per book in the U.S. and $1.25 per book in Canada.* I understand that accepting the 2 free books and gifts places me under no obligation to buy anything. I can always return a shipment and cancel at any time by calling the number below. The free books and gifts are mine to keep no matter what I decide.

Choose one: ☐ **Harlequin Special Edition** ☐ **Harlequin Heartwarming**
(235/335 HDN GRCQ)   **Larger-Print**
(161/361 HDN GRC3)

Name (please print)

Address   Apt. #

City   State/Province   Zip/Postal Code

Email: Please check this box ☐ if you would like to receive newsletters and promotional emails from Harlequin Enterprises ULC and its affiliates. You can unsubscribe anytime.

Mail to the Harlequin Reader Service:
IN U.S.A.: P.O. Box 1341, Buffalo, NY 14240-8531
IN CANADA: P.O. Box 603, Fort Erie, Ontario L2A 5X3

Want to try 2 free books from another series! Call 1-800-873-8635 or visit www.ReaderService.com.

*Terms and prices subject to change without notice. Prices do not include sales taxes, which will be charged (if applicable) based on your state or country of residence. Canadian residents will be charged applicable taxes. Offer not valid in Quebec. This offer is limited to one order per household. Books received may not be as shown. Not valid for current subscribers to the Harlequin Special Edition or Harlequin Heartwarming series. All orders subject to approval. Credit or debit balances in a customer's account(s) may be offset by any other outstanding balance owed by or to the customer. Please allow 4 to 6 weeks for delivery. Offer available while quantities last.

Your Privacy—Your information is being collected by Harlequin Enterprises ULC, operating as Harlequin Reader Service. For a complete summary of the information we collect, how we use this information and to whom it is disclosed, please visit our privacy notice located at corporate.harlequin.com/privacy-notice. From time to time we may also exchange your personal information with reputable third parties. If you wish to opt out of this sharing of your personal information, please visit readerservice.com/consumerschoice or call 1-800-873-8635. **Notice to California Residents**—Under California law, you have specific rights to control and access your data. For more information on these rights and how to exercise them, visit corporate.harlequin.com/california-privacy.

HSEHW22R2

HARLEQUIN
PLUS

Announcing a **BRAND-NEW** multimedia subscription service for romance fans like you!

Read, Watch and Play.

Experience the easiest way to get the romance content you crave.

Start your **FREE 7 DAY TRIAL** at www.harlequinplus.com/freetrial.

HARPLUS0822